D1006321

Lena,
the sea,
and me

Lena, the sea, and me

MARIA PARR

translated from Norwegian by Guy Puzey
illustrated by Lara Paulussen

CANDLEWICK PRESS

Text © 2017 Det Norske Samlaget, Oslo
Originally published as *Keeperen og havet* by Det Norske Samlaget, Oslo
Published in arrangement with Hagen Agency, Oslo
English language translation © 2020 Guy Puzey
Cover and interior illustrations © 2020 Lara Paulussen

First US edition 2021

Library of Congress Catalog Card Number pending
ISBN 978-1-5362-0772-9

21 22 23 24 25 26 LBM 10 9 8 7 6 5 4 3 2 1

Printed in Melrose Park, IL, USA

This book was typeset in Berkeley Oldstyle Book.

Candlewick Press
99 Dover Street
Somerville, Massachusetts 02144

www.candlewick.com

MIX
From responsible sources
FSC® C103098
www.fsc.org

A JUNIOR LIBRARY GUILD SELECTION

Contents

PART THREE: WINTER AND WAITING

PART FOUR: SPRING IS SPRUNG

Part One

Saltwater Summer

CHAPTER ONE

Jumping from the Breakwater

*T*he back door slammed shut, making our whole house shake. Then there followed an almighty crash and somebody shouting "Oh, fish cakes!"

I stumbled out of my attic bedroom onto the landing, still half-asleep. The rest of my family were already standing there with unbrushed hair and confused expressions. Minda, my big sister, only had one eye open. Dad looked like he hadn't worked out yet if he was a man or a duvet.

"Bang!" shouted my little sister, Krølla.

"What on earth was that?" asked Magnus, my big brother.

"Either there's been some kind of natural disaster," said Mom, "or Lena Lid's back from her vacation."

It wasn't a natural disaster. When I got to the bottom of the stairs, Lena, my best friend and dear neighbor, was standing there in the hallway.

"Hi, Trille," she sighed.

"Hi. What's that you've got there?"

"It's your present."

I rubbed my eyes. "Thank you. What is it?"

"A pile of sticks and broken glass, obviously! But it *was* a ship in a bottle."

Lena looked miserable.

"Maybe it can be fixed?" I suggested.

"Fixed?" said Lena. "It was supposed to be the best present ever. It can't be fixed! I really don't know how they managed to get that ship inside the bottle, Trille. The masts and sails were all up and were way wider than the neck."

Mom helped us clean up the shipwreck. She wanted to throw it away, but I gathered up all the bits of glass and wood in an ice-cream tub

4

and put it in my room. It was a present, after all.

Lena sat down at our breakfast table. She looked different, and I had to check carefully several times to see what had changed. She'd had her hair cut and gotten some multicolored braid things put into it. She'd gotten a suntan too. As for me, I felt a bit too much like my normal self, sitting there in the same old shorts I'd been wearing when she'd left. Our family hardly ever goes on vacation, or at least not abroad. We've got our farm and everything to look after. But Lena, that lucky sausage, she'd just spent two long weeks on Crete with her mom and her stepdad, Isak.

She'd drunk smoothies with little umbrellas in them, she told me while I ate my liver paste on bread. And she'd slept under only one sheet and swum in the warm sea. There were hundreds of little shops there, with millions of cool things she could get with her pocket money. Like that bottle. She'd had french fries for dinner every day. And it was so hot around lunchtime on Crete that it was almost like standing next to a Midsummer bonfire the whole time.

"Smoking haddocks, you should've seen what it was like, Trille!"

"Yes," I said, carrying on munching.

It was annoying never having been to the Mediterranean. But I had something exciting to tell Lena too. I waited anxiously for her to ask if anything new had happened back here in Norway. But she didn't. On Crete there was a speedboat she'd taken to a little island, she told me, and her mom had tried being dragged along behind it with some kind of balloon in the air.

"Anyway, did I tell you how hot it was?" she asked.

I nodded. Lena went on about a stray dog called Porto, who might have had rabies, about some girls she'd played with—who hardly dared to do any balancing games at all—and about having pancakes for breakfast.

Eventually I couldn't wait any longer.

"I jumped off the highest part of the breakwater."

Lena finally stopped talking. She squinted at me suspiciously. "You're joking."

I shook my head. My neighbor got up. I could

quite clearly tell that this was one of those things she'd have to see before she could believe it. And see it she would!

"Thanks for the food," I called to Mom with my mouth full.

Then I grabbed my towel from where it was hanging on the banister.

The L-shaped breakwater in Mathildewick Cove is made of massive rocks and has a swimming area in the crook of its arm. In the winter, the storms blow in fine sand, which we use to make sandcastles and other fortifications. But when Lena went on vacation that summer, I'd been allowed to go with Minda and Magnus and their friends to the outside of the breakwater, where it's highest and the water below is deep and cold. It was almost like the beginning of a new life.

Lena's the champion of Mathildewick Cove when it comes to jumping off tall things. Nobody has less fear in their stomach. Or less sense in their head, as Magnus says. But even Lena's never jumped from the breakwater. She doesn't float very well.

"Throwing Lena into the fjord is more or less like dropping an anchor," says Grandpa.

It was quite a big deal that there was something I could jump from that she couldn't. I could tell that Lena wasn't pleased.

There I was on the highest rock on the breakwater. It was the crack of dawn, and it was only sixty degrees outside.

"Are you sure you're psyched up enough for this?" Lena asked me seriously.

She was leaning over one of the other rocks, wearing her jacket and a Mediterranean scarf. I nodded. I'd jumped in the water lots of times while she'd been away. But it had always been at high tide. Now the tide was out, and it was farther to jump. I could see the bottom. The wind buffeted my swimming shorts. For a moment I wondered whether it was really worth it. But then I saw Lena, back from Crete, leaning over the rock and not believing I could do it.

I closed my eyes and took a deep breath. One. Two. THREE!

Ker-splash! came the sound as I hit the water, and then *sworlsh* as the bubbling surface closed over my head. The first time I'd gone down into the deep like this, I'd thought I was going to drown. Now I knew that all I had to do was thrash my legs around like crazy and hold my breath.

"*Phuh!*" I puffed as I shot back through the surface of the water and into the summer morning air.

Lena had climbed up onto the highest rock and was looking down at me skeptically. I smiled triumphantly. I'd shown her this time!

Next thing I knew, Lena was putting one foot in front of the other and slapping her hands against her face to psych herself up.

"*Ay-ay-aaaaaaaaaah!*" she howled.

Then she flew through the air in her jeans, sweater, jacket, scarf, and sneakers.

Ker-splash!

It was only as she leaped from the breakwater that Lena properly landed home from her vacation. Talking about smoothies on Crete doesn't quite have the same shine to it when you've almost drowned in Mathildewick Cove. She resurfaced after what seemed like an endlessly long time and then disappeared again with a *bloop*.

If Grandpa hadn't come along with his fishing gaff, I don't know how it all would've ended. He used the long pole with the hook on its end to pull Lena ashore like a giant fish while she coughed and flailed around worse than ever.

"I did actually drown for a moment," Lena said afterward. "I saw an enormous light."

We'd drunk two mugs of Isak's special red-hot July cocoa, but Lena was still shaking like a lawn mower left running.

"*Pfft,*" I said. "You can't drown and still be alive. It was just the sun. That's what it looks like from underwater."

"You don't know what I saw! The sea in Mathildewick Cove is colder than iced tea. The people on Crete would seriously die if they went swimming here!"

I didn't say anything. It was where we'd always swum.

"Well," Lena went on, "never in my life am I going to jump from that breakwater again. Been there, done that."

She tilted her head back happily, downing the last few gulps of her cocoa.

CHAPTER TWO

The Crowd at Hilltop Jon's Farm

*W*hen Mom heard about us jumping in the water, she gave each of us a formidably large bucket.

"Anybody who's big enough to jump from the breakwater is big enough to start helping out a bit more. Don't come home until you've picked enough bilberries to fill these right up," she ordered.

Lena looked at the buckets in horror. "I'm not part of your family, Kari."

"Shall I remind you of that next time we're having pancakes with bilberry jam here and you suddenly pop in?" Mom asked her.

I could see that Lena was thinking about answering back, but even she wouldn't dare to defy Mom. My mother's as strict as an old headmistress these days. Magnus secretly calls her "the Dictator." Lena says it's hardly surprising that Mom is so strict. She thinks things in the Danielsen Yttergård family are completely out of control. Minda and Magnus slam the doors so hard that our house is permanently trembling. And Krølla goes on and on so much that sometimes we could do with helmets to shield our heads.

"And then there's you, a lazy so-and-so always drifting off in your own world and never clearing away your plate after dinner. It's no wonder Kari has to sort you all out. It's just a shame that innocent people have to suffer when all they've done wrong is live in the house next door."

As for Lena, she's pleased she can relax with her own peaceful family. Things have calmed down at their house since she and her mom got Isak. He putters around with his ruffled hair and never gets mad. I wonder if he's so calm because he's a doctor. Maybe he's so used to illness and drama that living with Lena is no stress at all. Sometimes Lena calls him "Dad," but when she does, she says it quickly and seems a bit embarrassed, almost as if she's afraid he'll disappear if he hears that word.

By the time we reached the forest where the bilberries grow, up behind Hilltop Jon's farm, we'd walked off the cold from our swim. Lena stuck her head down into her bucket.

"Child labor!" she yelled with all her might. "There's an echo in here, Trille," she added. "Kari might as well have given us a whole bathtub to fill up."

I sat down by a bilberry bush and started to pluck the berries off the stalks. The sun's rays sneaked their way between a thousand leaves, making a polka-dot pattern on my T-shirt. Lena sat a short distance away, throwing pine cones.

For a brief moment, everything was lovely and quiet, like a summer's day ought to be, until she said, "One measly little brother, Trille. Is that too much to ask, do you think? Honestly?"

My best friend isn't a person who wishes for

things. She just decides how things are going to be. And two years ago, as soon as her mom had married Isak, Lena had made up her mind that they were going to have a baby, and that it was going to be a brother.

"It'll take a little while," she'd told Grandpa and me, "but soon I'll have a brother, who'll cry, poop, and look like me."

Lena was positively certain about it, and Grandpa and I were so used to things turning out as Lena wanted that we'd practically taken this brother for granted right away. But now two long years had passed. Lena and I were about to start our last year at primary school, and there was still no sign of so much as one of that brother's little toes over in the house next door.

"Babies don't just turn up when you want them to," I said. "Mom told me."

"What does your mom mean by that? You've got so many brothers and sisters that you can't move without crashing into somebody whenever you enter or leave a room."

I kept on picking berries. After a while, Lena ran

out of pine cones to throw, so she started pulling up clumps of moss instead. She laid them neatly in her bucket, and when it was almost full, she started picking berries with me.

"Lena," I sighed.

"One full bucket in no time at all. You should do the same, Trille. Nobody will notice."

"Yes, they will," I said. "They'll notice when they start taking the berries out and cleaning them."

"Yes, but I won't be there then," Lena assured me. "Shh, what was that?"

Desperate whimpers had suddenly pierced the quiet summer air of the forest. We spun around and peered through the trees. We couldn't see anything to start with, but then the whimpering came again.

"It's a dog!" Lena shouted, rushing toward it. "It's got its leash stuck! Poor thing."

Imagine finding a dog in the middle of the forest! It would've been one thing finding Labben or Aiko or Brandy, or one of the other dogs from the local area, but it wasn't any of them. It was a brand-new dog that neither Lena nor I had seen before. He had brown fur that shone beautifully in the sun, and he was looking at us with sad eyes.

"I think it's a sign," Lena said solemnly as we carefully freed him. "I think this is a dog that's come here to Mathildewick Cove to stay. In that case, I can always wait another year for a brother. We might even have too much on our hands as it is now . . ."

I looked at the dog's long leash. "Somebody owns him, Lena."

Lena didn't answer.

"Come on, boy!" she called.

Then she ran out of the forest and through the knee-high grass of Hilltop Jon's field — running backward for a bit and then turning again — all the while laughing at her new playmate. Lena was well suited to having a dog.

But her joy didn't last long. At Hilltop Jon's farm was a massive white van with a whole bunch of people standing around it.

"Haas!" they all shouted.

The dog raced off, dragging Lena, who fell right

17

over into a big, muddy tire track and lost hold of the dog's leash. When she got back up, she looked like something the dog had left behind. For several seconds she stood glowering at the people below, her arms sticking rigidly out from her sides. Then she marched on down.

"You don't take very good care of your dog!" she told them furiously.

The people stared at us, clearly terrified, especially of muck-covered Lena. I moved toward them nervously. At the back of the group I saw a girl who looked almost like sunshine. She had a cloud of blond curls around her head, and she smiled shyly as she scratched the dog behind his ears.

Then they started speaking in English. I'm much better at English than Lena. She can't see why she should have to learn English when she can already speak Norwegian. Although now she's been to Crete, perhaps she can see the point of it.

Before I could say anything, she'd beaten me to it.

"The dog was stucked in a tree!" Lena didn't know you say "stuck" in English.

"Ah! Thank you, thank you!" said a man who appeared to be the father of the family.

Lena stared at him angrily. She looked extremely dangerous as she stood there, dripping with mud.

"The ferry is that way!" she told them bluntly, pointing. "Come on, Trille."

I felt embarrassed. I smiled at the girl with the blond curly hair and followed Lena.

"Pickled herring, these tourists," she fumed, speaking in Norwegian again. "Always getting in a jam. Imagine being so lost that you end up driving all the way up here. They should have hazard lights stuck on them, the whole lot."

CHAPTER THREE

The Message in a Bottle

*L*ena said that she'd had enough of dry land, so the next day we decided to launch a message in a bottle. We used to send out loads of messages in bottles. This summer we'd only launched a couple: one from the ferry across the fjord and another from the breakwater. But Mathildewick Cove seemed to reel the bottles back in. They always ended up drifting onto one of the beaches by our house, and then people made fun of us. A proper message in a bottle was supposed to reach Shetland or Iceland. Or Crete, of course.

We'd gotten ourselves ready to leave at five o'clock in the morning. Grandpa was going all the way out to the small island of Kobbholmen to pull in a fishing line that had been out overnight, and he was letting us come too.

"Can't it go any faster, this boat of yours?" Lena asked as soon as we'd put out to sea. "When I went to Crete, I went on a speedboat that—"

"When you went to Crete indeed, you little madam!" said Grandpa. "Do you think this is just any old boat?"

He struck his fist against the side of the cabin.

I don't think there's anybody more fond of their boat than Grandpa. His boat's called *Troll*. Grandpa's always had her.

"Can't you at least get an engine with a bit more horsepower for this old *Troll* of yours?" Lena moaned. "It's going to take us all day to get far enough out."

"I've got all day," Grandpa replied.

I sat down on the deck. Imagine if our bottle really did manage to cross the sea. We'd written a message in English with our names, where we lived,

21

and a telephone number. We'd even put in a picture of ourselves. If somebody in another country found it, maybe they'd invite us to visit them.

"People from other countries are really cool," said Lena. "When I went to Crete . . ."

Grandpa and I exchanged a look and rolled our eyes.

"That's it. I can't be bothered sitting around here like a sea snail all day," Lena suddenly said behind me. Then she threw the bottle overboard with all the strength she could muster.

"Lena!" I shouted angrily. "We've only just come out onto the fjord."

My best friend gazed mournfully at the bottle. It bobbed up and down a little in the water and started gently drifting back inland in the breeze.

"Maybe I should jump in and get it back," she suggested.

"No, thank you, Lena Lid," said Grandpa. "I need my fishing gaff for other things today."

Lena flung herself down dramatically on the deck next to me. "Am I seriously going to be held hostage

22

on this boat for the rest of the day? Have we got any cookies?"

We chugged along the shores of the fjord until the sea opened up ahead of us. Out there, the swells rocked us like a great lullaby, and all the noise from the shore was left behind. My frustration about the bottle disappeared.

"Shetland's straight that way," I told Lena, pointing to where the ocean met the sky. "And there's Kobbholmen."

The small, dark island lay all alone amid the blue water. All that stood there was a lonely lighthouse.

"Is the island deserted?" Lena asked.

"Well, it is these days," said Grandpa. "But people used to live there in the past."

Lena and I looked at the little island and the peaceful lighthouse. Imagine living there, in the middle of the sea. As we came closer, we could see a house and a shed too. Small patches of grass came into view among the dark rocks.

Grandpa stood still for a time. He was looking at Kobbholmen as well.

"You know, your grandmother grew up out here, Trille," he said after a while.

"Huh?"

Grandpa nodded and began to maneuver the boat toward a buoy that was swaying in the sea a short distance away.

"You have a grandmother?" Lena asked, astonished. "Where have you been keeping her?"

"She's dead," I said. "She died when Dad was little."

"Oh."

Lena didn't say any more. She just stared at the lighthouse, deep in thought.

Grandpa moved calmly as he prepared to draw in the fishing line, as he'd done so many times before. He doesn't speak about my grandmother very often. But we always take two bunches of flowers when we go to the churchyard cemetery. One for Auntie Granny's grave, and one for Granny's. Auntie Granny was Grandpa's sister. My real granny's grave has a small round gravestone that looks different from the others. At the bottom, it says: *Sadly missed.*

I kept looking at Kobbholmen. It was as if a light had started shining around the island and the lighthouse. To think that my grandmother had grown up there. Had her father been the lighthouse keeper?

"Look out," said Grandpa as he started the winch.

The machine screeched and shook a little, then it started reeling in the line. Line fishing is an adventure. You never know what you'll find hanging on the hooks, and Grandpa always catches some fish. Nobody knows the fishing grounds around here better than he does. Once, when he was young, he caught a halibut that was bigger than he was: I've seen a picture of it. I dream of that happening again. That's why I always lean right over the side of the boat when we reel in the line. Grandpa lets me. He's not strict when we're out at sea. The only thing he looks out for is that we don't fall against the winch, as that's how Uncle Tor lost half a finger when he was little. Dad's always nagging Grandpa to install an emergency stop button on the winch. It's supposed to be a requirement, Dad says. But nobody gets to tell Grandpa what to do at sea. If somebody tries to tell him what to do with his boat, there's no way he'll do it.

"It's better to teach the young ones to be careful," he says, in answer to Dad.

Lena and I leaned as far as we dared over the side of the boat, telling Grandpa every time we saw a fish approaching the surface. About halfway along the line, we saw something big and slippery writhing in the dark water.

"It's a megafish!" Lena yelled. "Oh, holy mackerel. It's a megafish, Lars. Reel her in!"

An enormous cod smacked onto the deck. Lena howled with delight and started jumping up and down like a yo-yo.

"Next time you come," said Grandpa, "we'll try a halibut line." He laughed and rubbed his hands together. "Then the little lass from next door will see a real fish! That's if you can be bothered to come on this old *Troll* again."

"Bothered?" Lena put one foot on the cod, as if it were a dragon she'd just slain. "Actually, I may very well become a fisherwoman when I'm older," she said.

"Aren't you going to be a goalkeeper?" I asked as I fetched Grandpa's knife.

"Yes, but I've got to have something to fall back on when I hang up my gloves."

We didn't see the message in a bottle on our way back, and we had plenty of time to look for it, as Grandpa wanted to set a herring net before we returned to shore.

"Mark my words, Trille," said Lena. "Soon somebody will be calling from Spain wanting to speak to us!"

But nobody did call from Spain. Something else happened altogether. And it happened that very same evening.

*   *   *

I was lying on the sofa, reading, when the doorbell rang. I heard Krølla running for her life so she'd get to open the door, and I was quite stunned when she yelled that there was somebody to see me. Who could it be? Lena never rings the doorbell.

When I reached the door, I was struck speechless. The dog from the forest was sniffing inquisitively at my socks, and there, on the bottom step, stood the sunshine girl.

"I found this," she said cautiously, passing me the bottle.

CHAPTER FOUR

Birgit

*W*hat do you mean 'moved here'?" Lena whispered as she stared skeptically at the girl standing in our yard.

"The family with the dog have moved here! They're from the Netherlands, and they're renting Hilltop Jon's house!"

"Is that allowed?"

"Of course it is. Hilltop Jon lives at the retirement home now. Come on!"

I dragged Lena with me down into our yard. "This is Lena," I announced eagerly in English.

"Hi. I'm Birgit," the girl said, clearing her throat

slightly and politely reaching out to shake Lena's hand.

"Huh?" said Lena sharply. She seemed a bit rattled.

"Her name's Birgit!" I said.

I hoped Lena might jump at the chance to use the English she'd recently learned on Crete to say something welcoming, but clearly not. She stared glumly at the dog instead. He gave her a friendly sniff, like all animals do when they meet Lena. I squirmed in the embarrassing silence.

"Um, do you want to build a floating thing with us tomorrow?" I eventually blurted out.

Lena stiffened beside me.

"Floating thing?" Birgit asked, slightly puzzled.

One evening earlier in the summer, while we were sitting on the balcony, drinking some coffee and having a snack, Dad and Uncle Tor had started chatting about when they were young and had built a raft that they sailed all the way across the fjord to town. They probably hadn't meant for Lena and me to overhear, as Dad's face took on a concerned expression when he realized that we were listening. They quickly moved on to talk about something else.

But it was too late. If Dad and Uncle Tor could cross the fjord on a homemade raft, then so could Lena and I. Since then, we'd been secretly gathering flotsam and jetsam all summer and hiding it in the old boat shed.

Now I stood there in the yard, trying to explain to Birgit what a raft was in English. The problem was that I couldn't remember the word "raft." I looked helplessly at Lena a couple of times, but she just stared fiercely back.

"It's a thing that . . . um . . . you float on it on the sea . . . um; it's a . . ."

"A raft," Lena said eventually, as if she couldn't stand listening to me fumbling anymore.

Birgit lit up. I pointed down across the fields to the old boat shed, so she'd understand where our stockpile was.

"OK," she said a little nervously. "Haas, *kom hier!*"

Then off she went, vanishing through the hole in the hedge, past Lena's house, and up onto the road, taking her curly blond hair and everything else with her.

Lena shot off across the yard like a soldier into battle. I ran after her.

"Has something happened?" asked Lena's mom, Ylva, as we came storming into the living room.

"Yes!" I shouted. "A girl's moved here, and she's the same age as us."

Ylva pushed her glasses up and stared at me. "A new girl?" She clearly couldn't believe it. "Will she be in your class?"

I nodded enthusiastically. It was a miracle.

"So now you won't be the only girl in your class, Lena!" Ylva said, all excited. "That'll be a nice change."

Lena looked like she'd taken a cream pie to the face.

"A nice change?" she roared. "I couldn't care less about a nice change! It was Trille and me who were supposed to build the . . . you know what, Trille. And it was a secret."

Ylva raised her eyebrows in suspicion. "What kind of secret?"

"Nothing," Lena said hastily.

"Nothing?"

"That's right. But anyway, it was me and Trille who were going to do it. Not some curlyhead from the Nuttylands who we don't even know!"

"I was only trying to be kind," I said.

"You're always trying to be kind, you are, like some kind of archangel! You're so kind that it makes me sick!" Lena shouted.

I stared at her, not believing what I was hearing.

"Lena Lid!" It's not very often that Ylva raises her voice. "Do you remember the day we moved to Mathildewick Cove?"

"No," Lena said stubbornly.

"Let me remind you, then," said a stern Ylva. "No more than an hour after we'd arrived, the doorbell rang. There was a *kind* boy at the door, wondering if you wanted to come out and play. Do you remember who it was?"

Lena closed her mouth and glanced quickly at me.

"Exactly," said her mom. "Now say sorry, and say it right away."

For a long moment, it was as if Lena had been switched to silent.

"Sorry," she eventually muttered. It sounded like

she'd had to drag the word out of her appendix.

"I'm sorry too," I said quickly. I knew I really shouldn't have told an outsider about our secret raft plan, but why did Lena always have to be so difficult?

"That blasted bottle," Lena mumbled. "Is Mathildewick magnetic or something?"

"Still, it was somebody from another country who found it," I said, trying to cheer her up.

In return, I got a sofa cushion in the face.

As I shuffled back home that evening, I had to stop and look out at the fjord. The flat sea was like a mirror below the evening sky. I felt an unfamiliar tingling at the bottom of my stomach. Might Birgit actually show up?

CHAPTER FIVE

An Angel in the Boat Shed

*B*efore we went down to the beach the next day, Lena did some research on the Netherlands. In other words, she asked Isak, the cleverest person in Mathildewick Cove.

"Jiminy monkfish, I don't need any books or Internet since that guy moved in. All I have to do is type in a search query and click on his belly button."

She gave me a short lecture while we organized our assembled junk and waited for Birgit. There are loads of people in the Netherlands, Lena told me, and large parts of the country are below sea level.

"Below sea level?"

"Yes, but they've built dikes to stop the water seeping in and flooding everything. Isak says it's a nice country. Plus they're extremely good at soccer."

That soccer fact had clearly made Lena look at the situation in a more positive light. She's the goalie on our soccer team. When she stands in goal, yelling out orders, she's in her element. As for me, I'm starting to get tired of soccer. I'm no good at it. Everybody in our class plays, but sometimes I think I should just give up.

When Birgit finally peered around the boat-shed door, Lena immediately started talking about soccer. She bombarded her with questions, but Birgit couldn't answer a single one of them.

"Sorry. I'm not really that interested in soccer," she apologized.

Lena stood speechless behind our collection of junk, brandishing a hammer. I was afraid the situation might get out of control, so I clapped my hands.

"Let's get building."

It was strange having somebody new involved in our project. I hardly dared to look at Birgit. It was almost like having an angel in the boat shed. When she lifted up a plank of wood, she did it carefully, as if she'd never done it before. Maybe she hadn't? Lena grappled with various pieces of driftwood and nails at a furious pace. The things Lena makes are rarely very pretty, but she usually manages to put them together, one way or another. I started to feel irritated that she wasn't showing the quiet Dutch girl more consideration.

Eventually Birgit mainly just watched. Did she think we were totally weird? I'd never thought that the things Lena and I do are strange. But now that thought was buzzing around my head the whole time. Did we seem childish?

"Lena," I whispered when we went out to fetch some more plastic drums. "Shouldn't we try to involve her a bit more?"

Lena looked at me as if I'd asked her to conjure up a town hall out of thin air. When she went back into the boat shed, she escorted Birgit up into the open loft and gave her a sheet, as well as Krølla's box of paints, which she'd somehow gotten hold of.

"You can paint the sail," she explained, and then climbed back down. "Pass me the hammer, Trille."

* * *

Although Birgit was painting up in the loft and we were downstairs putting the raft together, we found out a lot more about her that morning. Birgit's father was an author and was going to spend a year writing. Her mother was an architect, but she wanted to try something else for a while. They'd been dreaming for ages of living on a small farm in Norway. Birgit's two elder brothers would be going back to the Netherlands when school started. They were in high school.

Word of the Dutch girl's arrival had rushed through the cove like a gale, and when we went up to my house to eat lunch, one person after another seemed to casually drop by. Lena's mom came to buy some eggs, and my older siblings, who were always pretending not to care about anything these days, spent a long time searching for various items in the kitchen cupboards. Mom even put out a tub of chocolate spread, despite the fact it wasn't Saturday. I could feel the pride growing inside me. I was the one who'd found Birgit!

Eventually, Lena said "Ah-heeeemm!" and nodded in the direction of the boat shed.

We did the last bit of joining in the sunshine out on the foreshore. Birgit sat on a rock, watching. Was it really stupid making a raft? I don't normally make mistakes when hammering and so on, but that day I hurt my thumb twice. Luckily I managed to act as if nothing had happened.

When we'd finished, Birgit fetched the sail and rolled it out. Lena and I were speechless. She'd painted the sea and the sky, as well as the sun, and at the top she'd painted Lena and me as a couple of pirates. It was the best-looking thing made by somebody my age that I'd ever seen.

"Wow!" I said. "That's fantastic."

I stuck out my arms in amazement and turned toward Lena. She was gawking like a fish too, but then she slammed her mouth shut.

"Is it waterproof?" she asked, sticking to the practicalities.

CHAPTER SIX

The Launch — and a Wretched Big Brother

*T*hey'll be calling us for dinner soon," Lena grumbled. She seemed in a rush as she grabbed the raft from underneath and dug in her heels.

It didn't budge one inch. I pushed as hard as I could from behind. Birgit took hold of it on one side, but it was no use.

"Push from the back with Trille," Lena ordered. "Push hard."

Birgit carefully nudged the raft next to me.

"Come on, heave, for crying out trout!" Lena yelled.

I looked angrily at her. Getting angry helped.
It made us stronger, both Lena and me. The raft
scraped across the stones.

As soon as it got some water beneath it, the raft
let go of the ground and started gently and nimbly
swaying on the waves. Cautiously, we climbed
aboard, one by one.

Everything was fine for a couple of seconds, but
then we felt something give way. I moved over a
little so we wouldn't capsize.

"Help!" Birgit whispered, grabbing on to the mast.

First there was some bubbling around the boards,
then the water started washing across the wood
and wrapping mercilessly around our calves, until
eventually the whole raft hit the sandy bottom with
a sigh.

There we stood. All that was left sticking out of the
water was half of ourselves, half the mast, and the sail
floating on the surface and turning to watercolors.

"Wood's no good," said Lena from behind
clenched teeth.

Then we heard laughter from the shore.

Whenever I make a house of cards and it

collapses, or I make a raft and it sinks, Magnus appears like a genie from a bottle. I don't think I've ever once fallen off my bike without him seeing it. There he was now, leaning against the wall of the boat shed and slapping his thigh.

"Don't tell me that's supposed to be a raft. Don't say it! I'll die laughing," he said in between hiccups.

Lena jumped off. Our vessel rose from the bottom and almost floated up to the surface.

"Can't you see it's a submarine, you onion brain?" she shouted.

Then Magnus laughed so much he could hardly breathe.

Really? I thought. *He's almost sixteen. Can't he find other things to laugh at than his younger brother?* I felt embarrassed and looked at Birgit.

"I swear," Lena muttered. "I swear that by sunrise tomorrow, this idiot-proof raft will be afloat, and we'll be halfway to town."

When Lena swears something, it's going to happen. After dinner, we were back in the boat shed, making improvements. Birgit had gone home.

"It wouldn't have been safe enough even for just two people," I said when we'd managed to flip the raft over and had started to attach another layer of polystyrene foam.

Lena didn't answer. She just swung her hammer so hard that I was glad I wasn't a nail.

When I went back inside that evening, my head was a mess from spending the day in the boat shed, but there was a full symphony at home, as usual. Minda and Mom were arguing tooth and nail about some trip or other that Minda clearly wasn't being allowed to go on, Krølla was playing her recorder, and Magnus was sitting on a chair wearing earplugs. He chuckled when he saw me.

I slipped out through the door and down to Grandpa's apartment. When you're in there, the rest of my family are only a distant muffled noise. You can hear the clock ticking and the cat purring. It's almost like another world.

But that day the racket had spread into the basement too. I stopped halfway down the stairs when I heard Dad's angry voice.

"When will you get it into your stubborn head? You don't stand a chance in those overalls," he shouted.

"Uggh," Grandpa replied.

"Don't you 'uggh' me," said Dad. "We're worried about you!"

"Uggh," said Grandpa again. "If that's all you've got to worry about, then I hardly feel sorry for you."

I kept quiet as a mouse on the stairs so they wouldn't hear me.

"I've got a house full of half-crazy teenagers, but you're the worst of all!" Dad shouted. "And you're seventy-eight years old!"

"Precisely," said Grandpa. "Seventy-eight and old enough to make up my own mind. Get out of the way, lad."

I heard Dad's angry pacing and the clatter of Grandpa doing the dishes.

"Dad . . ." my father began again, in a softer tone.

But Grandpa cut him off. "Up you go, now, Reidar. You're making my plants wilt with all your shouting."

Then Dad came stomping up the stairs. He didn't even say hello as he went past.

"Were you arguing?" I asked anxiously when I got down to Grandpa.

"Uggh," Grandpa replied. "Your father wants me to start wearing some kind of massive survival suit when I'm out at sea." He wiped the countertop roughly with a cloth. "I've been wearing simple overalls my whole life, and I'm not about to start staggering around like an astronaut on my own boat."

"But . . ."

"People shouldn't worry so much about an old duffer like me. It doesn't matter much anymore, anyway."

"Doesn't matter? I don't want you to drown," I said.

"I'm not planning on drowning, Trille! I can look after myself. That's what I've always done."

He threw the cloth into the sink and found me some cookies.

"If I started wearing a survival suit, then your

father would want me to wear a life jacket on top, and if I wore a life jacket on top, then he'd want to tie inflatable rings to my hands. And if I had inflatable rings tied to my hands, then he would soon decide that I shouldn't be out at sea at all. Then I would definitely die."

I saw Grandpa in my mind's eye, wearing a survival suit with a life jacket and inflatable rings. On dry land.

"Doesn't Dad realize that you can look after yourself?"

Grandpa drummed his fingers on the table, as if the agitation from the argument had to get out somehow.

"He's always been scared that something might happen to me."

"Why?"

Grandpa sighed. "Well, I was all the children had left, you know, after we lost Inger."

Now he was talking about my grandmother again. I pictured the island and the lighthouse, and suddenly I had so many questions. But I didn't really know how to start.

"Did she have curly hair?" I eventually asked.

Grandpa looked at me in astonishment and then laughed a little.

"Curly hair? No, she didn't. But she was the only girl with short hair. Beat that, if you can. Anyway. What have you been up to all day? I can smell secret projects from miles away."

So I told Grandpa about the raft and Birgit and Lena. He's not the sort to tell or put a stop to crucial operations.

CHAPTER SEVEN

Do Ferries Have to Give Way?

*T*he wind came plunging down from the mountains, making small, choppy waves on the sea. It was the crack of dawn. We peeped out from behind the wall of the boat shed to see Grandpa and *Troll* just leaving the pier and setting off out to sea. For the first time, I felt a slight twinge inside. What if Grandpa really was too old now to fend for himself out there? Should I start going with him more often?

Birgit had her chin buried in the collar of her jacket. She looked nervous.

"It's a bit windy," I said.

Lena narrowed her eyes as she licked her forefinger and lifted it into the air.

"The wind's blowing straight toward town."

She'd taken the paddles from my punctured rubber dinghy. And three life jackets. There was nothing more to discuss. Soon we were each sitting on a fish box on board the raft. The sail was hoisted. You could see Lena's head and mine at the top. The rest was a blur of watercolors. The raft looked sturdy in some ways and wobbly in others. But the most important thing was that we were afloat. In just a few seconds we were out of the shallows and past the drop-off, where the water suddenly gets much deeper.

Lena and I paddled. Birgit held on tightly to the mast. I wished I could find a way to make her feel safe, but before I could think of anything, Lena started singing pirate songs. A little smile flashed across Birgit's face. It was so nice that I missed a paddle stroke.

Water kept on washing over our feet, and the raft was rocking more than was comfortable. A little voice inside told me that this wasn't the smartest thing we'd ever done. But Lena was right about one thing: the wind was certainly in our favor, blowing along the fjord and toward town. And it was too late to turn back. All we could do was keep a steady course and focus on our target. Dad and Uncle Tor had done it. I gulped and gave Birgit a smile of encouragement.

"Are you OK?"

"Mhm," she mumbled, just barely nodding.

"Ahoy!" yelled Lena. "There's the ferry. Good thing we didn't set off ten minutes later, or we'd have been smashed to pieces."

The ferry doesn't exactly go at breakneck speed. In fact, Lena and I have discussed many times how you'd have to search pretty far and wide to find anything as absurdly slow as that ferry. Lena's sure that it goes slow on purpose, just so that Dad — Able Seaman Yttergård — has time to have a coffee on each trip between selling the tickets. But today it looked different.

"Have they put on an extra engine or something?" Lena asked.

The ferry grew from being the size of a toy boat

to the size of a ferry in a bafflingly short time. It almost felt like it was aiming for us. I paddled as powerfully as I could. On the other side of the raft, Lena was paddling so quickly that anybody would have thought she was trying to make some kind of seawater eggnog.

"Aren't big boats supposed to give way to small ones?" she shouted furiously.

I let out a desperate groan. "It's the other way around, Lena!"

Birgit's face was completely white.

The ferry's massive bow started to look like the maw of a monster. I was sure this was going to end in disaster, and I began waving my arms desperately. At the last moment, the ferry blasted its horn and veered out of the way. Thank goodness!

"Holy halibut, they shouldn't be sleeping at the wheel up there! It would've been quite a scandal if they'd run over us!" Lena bellowed.

She shook her fist and was so furious that I realized she must have been really scared too.

* * *

But we weren't out of danger yet. The ferry's wake was bigger than our raft could stand. The first wave swept right over our entire craft, washing two of our fish boxes into the sea. The second one made the raft tilt so much we almost lost our balance. And the third was so powerful that Lena slid with a scream into the water. When I threw myself across the raft to rescue her, yet another wave came and tipped me into the sea as well.

"We're shipwrecked!" Lena shouted from inside her enormous life jacket.

She kicked and struggled to get back on board. With Birgit's help, she eventually managed it, but her lips had already turned blue by then. Luckily her rage kicked in.

"Son of a sea bass, I'm going to crush that ferry the next time I see it," she said, shivering. "I'm going to —"

"Can you help me first?" I shouted.

I'd never been in the sea fully dressed before. Even though I was wearing a life jacket, it felt like the ocean was dragging me down, trying to pull me under into the darkness below. I was frightened and kept kicking away in the cold water.

Birgit and Lena tried to spread their weight so we wouldn't tip over too much when I pulled myself aboard. Something was creaking perilously in this raft we'd designed. One of the pieces of polystyrene came loose, and then another. The whole thing was disintegrating! I was left clinging on between one of the floating fish boxes and the crumbling raft, and I was just about to start panicking when we realized that the ferry had stopped.

Shivering and speechless, we saw they were sending out one of their lifeboats. Lena groaned as she hid her face behind her hands.

"If that's your dad coming to fish us out, then I think I'd prefer to stay here and drown!"

Of course it was Dad. Oh, how he shouted at us! He was like a soccer coach from town. Halfway through the worst volley, he put his arms around me and hugged me so tightly I thought I would suffocate. But then he started again. We could have drowned! Or gotten hypothermia! Were we planning on growing up and behaving like normal people sometime soon? And had we considered that the ferry was full of cars and passengers going to work? Now the whole timetable was a gigantic mess because we'd been thrashing around like befuddled seagull chicks straight in the path of the ferry. In the middle of the fjord!

But when he realized that there were three of us, he was completely derailed. Dad hadn't been at home when Birgit had visited.

"Have you taken a hostage?" he asked.

"Yes," Lena grumbled. "She's from the Netherlands. We were taking her back."

CHAPTER EIGHT

The Day on Kobbholmen

*B*irgit kept her distance after that. We later found out it was because her parents thought we must be trouble. They were probably right. The story of the shipwrecked raft quickly spread all across the area, and for the first time in my life, I felt ashamed. To think that I'd invited Birgit to join in with something so stupid! What a muttonhead I'd been! I looked up toward Hillside and wondered what she was doing. Summer vacation was almost over. I should've been running around from morning until evening enjoying the last of my freedom. Instead

I felt bored. It was as if Mathildewick Cove had become too small.

"You're all wound up, Trille," Mom said desperately one afternoon. "Go out and get some fresh air."

Out, out, out. We always had to go out. Couldn't she make some toasted buns and play a game with me instead? I walked down to the sea, feeling annoyed.

Ever since I was little, I've gone to Grandpa's boat shed to help him with things. We disentangle nets, prepare lines, and clean fish. Soon I'll know how to do most things by myself. Grandpa's passing his knowledge down to me. Sometimes when I coil a rope or put the knife in its place on the beam, I feel that I've done it just like Grandpa. The old men at the shop call me "Mini-Lars." I probably take after Grandpa more than I take after my dad.

So I plonked myself on an upside-down fish tub in the boat shed. Grandpa glanced at me and pretended not to hear me sighing.

"I promised that little lass from next door we'd

set a halibut line before the summer was over. Maybe we could do it tomorrow?" he suggested, digging out a large box of tangled fishing line.

I shrugged and lifted up one of the hooks.

Cool summer rain began to dance on the boat shed roof. I heard Dad shouting something in the distance and Minda answering. Grandpa worked away calmly next to me with his big, tanned hands.

"Have you always been like you are now, Grandpa?"

Grandpa briefly shook a tangled piece of line, and a hook came loose. He put it in a wooden box.

"Old, gray-haired, and fond of fish?"

"No . . ."

We sorted out a few more hooks. I shifted nervously.

"Have you always been so . . . content?" I eventually asked.

Grandpa looked at me, a little surprised. "Mm, yes. Except for getting in the odd bit of trouble in my youth."

"Trouble?"

"Well, you know the sort of thing. A bit of ants in

my pants and some argy-bargy. Just ask Thunderclap Kåre."

He laughed, but I wondered what Thunderclap Kåre had to do with anything.

"But I've been really lucky. I'm healthy, I've got a family, I have a boat and plenty of time on my hands."

He shook the tangled line patiently.

"But Granny died," I blurted out.

Grandpa stowed away another hook.

"Yes." His hands stopped. I held my breath. "But I was lucky to be married to her first. That was the luckiest part of all, Trille lad."

He stowed the last hook in the box.

"Make sure you bring Lena tomorrow."

I nodded.

The sky was light blue and hazy when we put out to sea the next day. There wasn't a puff of wind in the air, the seabirds sailed silently above us, and it was as calm as I'd ever seen it out by Kobbholmen. Even Lena was quiet as hook after hook of shiny herring bait plopped into the water and vanished into the darkness below.

"Those halibut are going to have a first-class meal down there now," she cackled as the last bit of herring disappeared from sight. "Delicious but deadly."

I could see that Grandpa was laughing inside. He likes being around Lena.

I peered through the haze at the lighthouse and the dark island. Lena did the same. Then suddenly she asked, "Can we go ashore?"

Grandpa threw the fishing buoy overboard and spat at it for luck, as fishermen have always done here. "Well, I was thinking we could do some fishing while we wait," he said.

"How many freezers have you got?" Lena said. "Don't they ever get full?"

Grandpa took off his cap and scratched his head. "You certainly have a way with words, Lena Lid. Maybe we will pay a visit to Kobbholmen, then."

As soon as I set foot on the old pier, my whole body began to tingle. A brand-new place to explore! Lena and I set off toward the center of the island. There were concrete steps and old railings everywhere.

Our hands were drawn to the black rocks, warmed by the sun. We ran like crazy and climbed like mad.

"Hey, those look like eggs," said Lena when we'd scrambled up one of the highest crags and were looking down at a small bay full of round gray boulders.

It was a bit hard to get down there, but we were soon on the beach, crouching and patting the smooth rocks. Only the sea could make something that smooth. All the edges and chipped parts had been ground away. I imagined how the roaring waves had washed over the shore right here, knocking and rolling the boulders against one another over thousands of years. I felt warm and happy as I sat down on one of the biggest ones and stared out to sea. Pink thrift flowers waved in the faint breeze, and the white lighthouse towered over us.

"Are you coming, then?" said Lena.

We went over to the old house. The windows were hidden behind great wooden boards, and the door was locked. How long had it been since people had made coffee, had a nap, or done the dishes inside those walls? Lena managed to find an opening in the shed, behind a rotten plank of wood. It was dark and silent inside, with only narrow bands of light coming in.

She knocked on the woodwork as she inspected the whole room, and I suddenly noticed that she had grown taller. When she stood on her tiptoes, she could reach the ceiling. Lena's always been a bit shorter than me, but now she wasn't anymore. What if the others in my class had grown just as much over the summer, and I was the only one who was exactly the same height as before? I took a nervous step in the dark. It was only gossip, but Lena had heard that Kai-Tommy's voice was changing.

"They used to keep chickens in here," said Lena, pointing behind some wire netting.

"Hmm," I said, remembering something Dad had said one Sunday at home when he was making chicken fricassee: "This used to be your grandmother's favorite dish, Trille. Chicken fricassee and homemade red-currant squash to drink."

When we got back to the lighthouse, I saw the two

red-currant bushes in a warm spot next to the steps.

And up on the steps themselves was Grandpa. He'd kicked off his clogs and rolled up the trouser legs on his overalls, his white shins reflecting the sunlight.

Lena let out a shriek and covered her eyes. "I'm snow-blind!"

"Oh, be quiet, you!" Grandpa tossed us our packed lunches. He looked happy as he wiggled his toes.

"I definitely could've lived here," said Lena, plonking herself down on the bottom step.

"Oh, it's good on Kobbholmen today, but my, how the wind can blow out here."

"So was Trille's granny actually a lighthouse keeper?" Lena fished out a piece of bread as big as her face.

"No, her father was the lighthouse keeper," said Grandpa.

"Was she living out here when you fell in love with her?" Lena went on.

I glanced up at Grandpa. Was he getting fed up with all these questions about Granny? No. He looked happy.

"Well, I'd say she was living here when she fell in love with me!"

"Pfft," said Lena. "You're just boasting."

Then Grandpa told her gruffly that he had once been young and handsome too, whether we believed it or not.

"But I wanted to be an oceangoing mariner and sail to Shanghai and Liverpool and Baltimore. I wasn't about to fritter my time away in Mathildewick Cove and get married. Not on your nelly!"

He shook his head. "You two should've seen the long line of girls I've turned down in my life!"

"Yes, I'd like to have seen that," Lena said dryly. "Was Trille's granny in that line too?"

Grandpa smiled and looked out to sea.

"Yes and no," he murmured.

A gentle breeze began to rustle softly through the grass around the steps.

"We'd better get in the boat, young 'uns!"

"How do you know where to put these fishing lines, anyway?" Lena asked as we approached the buoy.

Grandpa laughed. Nobody will ever share the

secrets of how to find their best fishing spots!

"Inger," he said. "She was the one who showed me the best places out here. Goodness knows I could've kept close to the shore, fishing for kelp cod with Thunderclap Kåre and Co., but that wouldn't have been as much fun. Can you reach the buoy, Trille?"

We didn't catch any halibut, but we got a whole heap of tusk and cod. Grandpa looked strong as he hooked them with his fishing gaff and pulled them onto the boat. Maybe I wasn't as much like Grandpa as I'd thought, I wondered, feeling sad in a strange and new way. Girls weren't going to be lining up anywhere near me.

That evening, I cycled to the churchyard alone. Lena's often tried to scare me off from going there. She tells me about ghosts and grave robbers and Satanists and goodness knows what else. But I've always liked it there. This time it felt especially good to open the gate and walk in under the cool trees. My head was pounding from too much sun and sea.

I walked past Auntie Granny's grave and over to the small, round gravestone on the other side of the churchyard. *Inger Yttergård*, it said in gold writing. *Born May 6, 1933, died November 22, 1968.* What was she like, I wondered, this lady who had been married to Grandpa? Mom had told me that she'd died of cancer. My heart felt crushed when I thought about it. Grandpa had lost her, and so had Dad. Long before I was here. Is it possible to miss somebody you've never met? I patted the smooth stone, and suddenly my fingertips remembered something. I took a step backward and looked again at the gravestone, which I'd always thought was a little odd.

It was a boulder from Kobbholmen.

Part Two

Autumn Uproar

CHAPTER NINE

Kai-Tommy's Voice

*A*utumn was on its way. From my window, I could see *Troll* chugging cheerily out across a grayish-blue late August fjord. The school bell was about to start controlling my life, but Grandpa could carry on like before: fishing, drinking coffee, and having a peaceful time.

As I turned away from the window and lifted up my backpack, I realized that I was looking forward to school a bit after all. Today I would get to see Birgit again. For the first time in my life, I spent a long time standing in front of the closet, pondering what to wear. I didn't think any of my clothes were especially cool. I pinched some of the hair wax that Magnus keeps in the bathroom.

Usually Mom gets up before me, but that morning, on the first day back at school, she was still sleeping.

"Is she ill?" Magnus asked as he rummaged in the fridge.

"She's just tired," said Dad. There was a wrinkle on his brow.

I packed my lunch as quick as the wind and leaped into my boots so I could walk with Minda and Magnus to their bus stop.

"Minda, did you notice that Dad was worried?" I scurried along beside her.

"Dad's always worried."

"But Mom usually comes to say goodbye and tell us to have a good day," I said.

Minda stopped. "Have you ever thought that Mom isn't just there to get up and say goodbye to you, Trille? Maybe she'd like to sleep in for once. Maybe she's got her own life to get on with!"

I opened my mouth to say something.

"And if you don't stop wearing those boots to

school soon, there'll be no hope for your social life," she finished, and ran off to the bus.

I watched her go. What was wrong with wearing wellies to school? It was raining, after all! Then somebody grabbed my hood, almost strangling me.

"Why hello, you little gnome. Ready for our last year at primary? We're going to rule the school," said Lena, grinning.

Luckily, she was wearing wellies too.

Our cove is a bit out of the way, so it's a fair distance to walk to school. The first thing we come to is the road that leads up to Hillside, and after that there's quite a long stretch with the sea on one side and thick spruce forest on the other. I've lost count of the times Lena's disappeared up into the forest and frightened me out of my wits by jumping out at me farther on. But today she walked with me all the way. We didn't see Birgit.

"Did you know that Ellisiv's bought this place?" Lena said as we passed the lone red cottage on the road between the forest and the ferry landing.

"Yes, Mom told me."

"Maybe we should start walking to school with our teacher."

Lena looked like she wasn't sure whether her suggestion was a good or bad idea. She's very fond of Ellisiv.

The ferry landing was deserted, and the little shop wasn't open yet. The local teenagers normally hang out there in the afternoons. They ride their mopeds and sit around on the tables.

"Sitting there and gaping at the ferry is enough to kill anybody's soul," Lena said once. "Just look at Magnus."

It wasn't exactly a nice thing to say about my elder brother. But she had a point.

Kai-Tommy was hanging over his handlebars as we entered the school playground, and he shouted something at us. His voice was deep like a grown man's, but it broke at the end, and the last words sounded like seagulls screeching.

"His voice *is* changing." Lena was impressed and shocked at the same time.

"Are you two hard of hearing?" he asked, skidding to a stop in front of us. He was wearing new black sneakers and a cap and hoodie instead of a bike helmet.

"I didn't catch what you said because of your new voice," Lena said frankly.

Kai-Tommy jumped off his bike. "I said: Have you seen Birgit?"

Huh? Had Kai-Tommy met Birgit?

He had. It turned out he and Halvor had spent a great deal of time with Birgit over the past few days. They'd been swimming at the ferry landing, and they'd even been to visit her up at Hillside. It took all my strength not to let my jaw drop. I was the one who'd found Birgit first! Why on earth would she spend time with Kai-Tommy and Halvor? They were the two biggest idiots in the whole school!

Lena told Kai-Tommy that we hadn't seen Birgit since the great shipwreck a few weeks ago.

"We were at death's door, and Trille's dad was so furious that I think she was scared away."

Did Lena always have to blabber away like that? I didn't want Kai-Tommy to know anything. Not about Birgit, not about me, and certainly not about Dad.

What a terrible start to everything. Lena stayed there talking with Kai-Tommy, probably because he'd gotten such a wacky voice. I shuffled off inside, looking like an idiot in my boots. It was silent and deserted in the corridor outside the classrooms. Schoolbags were strewn everywhere. The last remains of the summer ran off me. I put my back against the wall and slid down. By now Grandpa would be somewhere out at sea. And I was stuck here.

"Are you all right?"

I hadn't seen her amid all the bags. It was almost like she was hiding. Birgit. She was even speaking Norwegian now.

"Erm, yes," I said, blushing. "And you?"

She shrugged slightly. I don't know precisely what I'd been expecting, but when Kai-Tommy said they'd been hanging out with her, I'd assumed that she would probably be all stupid and arrogant now. But she was exactly the same. A cautious smile and a soft voice. Was it possible to be like that and yet still be friends with Kai-Tommy?

By the time the bell rang, the crazy morning had gotten better. I'd spoken with Birgit for quite a while. I'd told her about Ellisiv and about the school and our class. Birgit asked if we'd made any more rafts, which I flatly denied. Then she smiled, and my head went all fuzzy.

CHAPTER TEN

Lena and I Go for Music Lessons

*O*n Tuesday, it was time for our music lessons to start up again. We'd been having them for the past two years: Lena was learning the keyboard and I was learning the piano. I'd explained to Mom that I'd prefer to play the drums, but for some reason or other that appeared to be out of the question.

"I have a feeling that I might have a talent for the drums," I told Lena.

Our lessons were one after the other this year too.

"You don't have a talent for the piano, anyway," she

replied, whirling the plastic bag with her keyboard book in it around her head like a sledgehammer.

"I'm better than you," I mumbled.

My best friend is absolutely terrible at the keyboard. Ylva loves music and plays all kinds of instruments, but Lena hasn't inherited a single ounce of musicality. Sometimes when I've been listening to Lena mangling a song on the keyboard, I think that father of hers, who ran off before she was born, must have been completely tone-deaf. But I haven't told Lena, of course. I think Ylva harbors a hope as deep as the forest that her daughter's got a musical side hidden away somewhere. She's very keen for Lena to learn the keyboard, anyway.

Mr. Rognstad, our teacher, doesn't show much understanding for people who can't play. It's as if he thinks our lack of talent is on purpose. Lena behaves very strangely when she's having her keyboard lesson. She looks at the floor and turns into a little jellyfish mumbling "yes" or "OK" and nothing else, no matter how unfair he's being.

Lena, who always speaks straight from the heart!
I can't get my head around it.

"I'm going to quit this year," Lena said now.

"What about your skis?" I asked. Ylva had
promised her new skis for Christmas if she kept up
the lessons for another year.

"Ugh, there'll probably be just as little snow this
year as there was last year. I hate music lessons.
I can't keep on doing things I hate."

"I can't stop. Mom says—"

"Trille." Lena paused. "Have you ever thought
that maybe sometimes you're right and your mom's
wrong?"

I sank into my jacket collar and shook my head.
But now that Lena mentioned it, it struck me that
there were a whole host of things Mom had said and
done recently that I didn't agree with at all.

"Do you think my mom's been a bit strange
recently?" I asked.

"Strange? She's totally cuckoo, Trille."

"What do you think is wrong with her, then?"

"Menopause."

It was as if Lena had been waiting for me to ask about Mom.

"Is that an illness?"

"Not exactly an illness."

It depended on how you looked at it, according to Lena. Some call it The Change. All women have to go through it when they reach the age where they can't have children anymore. Their bodies change and start to become like old ladies' bodies. But before they finish changing, there's a lot of sweating and nerves and miserable stuff.

"Some of them become fat, and others just feel fed up. I think your mom's got both sides of it."

I was shocked. Poor Mom!

"In that case, I think it's best I choose another time to stop learning the piano," I said.

"That's probably wise," said Lena. "But I can stop. My mom's from a different generation than yours."

And then we'd arrived. Lena slowly opened the door to the music school corridor.

"I hope Kai-Tommy's still before me, like last year."

Kai-Tommy's even worse than Lena. For a while, when Lena and he were more enemies than ever, she had insisted on arriving for her music lesson a quarter of an hour early so she could stand in the corridor and take joy in all the slipups and sighs coming from inside.

But today there was a surprise. Fantastic piano music was flowing out from behind the closed classroom door.

"That's definitely not Kai-Tommy," Lena declared. She listened to the piano trills, clearly downhearted. "Maybe that's Mr. Rognstad himself playing," she said hopefully.

Then the door opened, and out came Birgit.

"Hi!" she said, smiling in surprise. She was carrying a pile of sheet music under her arm.

I felt warm, then cold, then warm again. Could she play the piano too?

"See you next week, Birgit," said a happy Mr. Rognstad. Then he turned toward Lena and seemed to deflate a little. "Back again this year, Miss Lid?"

I could see that Lena was about to give one of her typical replies, but then she closed her mouth. I don't know which of them sighed loudest as they disappeared into the classroom.

"How was it?" I asked Lena on the way home.

She had looked even gloomier than usual when she'd finished her lesson.

"All right."

My lesson had been just all right too. But now it was going to be another kettle of fish. I couldn't keep playing like a porpoise if Birgit might be listening. Just think, now I could chat with her in the corridor every Tuesday. I could teach her Norwegian words.

"Maybe we should ask Birgit if she'd like to go with us next time," I said.

Lena kicked a stone, which shot off an endless distance down the road. "Didn't I tell you that I'm going to stop going, you sea cucumber?"

But the next Tuesday, Lena was waiting with her keyboard bag once again.

"Weren't you going to quit?" I asked her, surprised.

"Do you think I can afford my own skis?" she snapped, glancing over at the junction of Hilltop Jon's road, where Birgit stood waiting.

CHAPTER ELEVEN

The New Soccer Coach

*T*hanks to Birgit, my music lessons were going much better than I'd thought. But soccer was ten times worse.

"You're kidding," Lena mumbled as we arrived at our practice. She propped her bike against the fence by the side of the field. "Where's Axel?"

Our old soccer coach — the one who'd discovered Lena's goalkeeping ability, and who was the nicest man in the world — was nowhere to be seen. Instead, Kai-Tommy's dad was standing there.

"Why would he bother to train us?" Lena whispered. "We're terrible."

When he was young, Ivar, Kai-Tommy's dad, used
to play in the first division. Kai-Tommy tells that
to anybody with ears to listen. Kai-Tommy's big
brother is also a real soccer talent. He plays for
a junior team in town and has started training
with their first team now and then. He's the one
their father's been focusing on all these years. On
the rare occasions he'd turned up at our games,
he didn't act like the other parents, cheering and
jumping up and down however well we were
playing. No, he kept totally silent with his eyes
picking up everything. Kai-Tommy worked like
crazy and shouted twice as much at the rest of us
when we were being useless, especially at me.

After one such game, when Kai-Tommy had
snarled at me that I belonged at under-tens level and
was a disgrace to the team, Lena had explained a
couple of things on the way home.

"Kai-Tommy's got a major inferiority complex
when it comes to soccer, Trille."

"What do you mean, an inferiority complex?"
I asked angrily. I hated Kai-Tommy so much right

then that steam was practically coming out of my ears. He'd almost made me cry!

"In Kai-Tommy's family, soccer is the most important thing in the world. His brother's really good, but Kai-Tommy's nothing special."

"He's the best on our team," I said harshly.

"*Pfft*," said Lena. "When he shouts and yells, then everybody thinks that. And he shoots hard. But he's got poor technical abilities."

Technical abilities? Where did Lena pick up all these words?

"But . . ." I began.

"Kai-Tommy's an average player, Trille. And you can bet that doesn't impress his dad."

Lena didn't say any more after that. But it made it easier to put up with all of Kai-Tommy's nonsense. When he shouted something angrily at me, all I had to think was that he had an inferiority complex. And poor technical abilities too.

But now, at practice that day, I could tell things were going to be different. Kai-Tommy's father stood in the middle of the field, in a black tracksuit, rolling a ball under one foot. He looked lethal.

Kai-Tommy swept back his bangs, making sure he looked good. I realized this inferiority complex was going to come out at every single practice now.

"I bet it's Axel's girlfriend who's made him stop coaching, so he can go with her to the café every single day instead," Lena grumbled.

We don't like our old coach's girlfriend. She's so pretty that Lena thinks it's made her crabby, and she doesn't know a thing about soccer, or about Axel really. We pictured Axel sitting in a deep café armchair in town while we were hopelessly stuck at practice.

"Oh well," said Lena, pulling on her goalkeeper's gloves. Clearly she wasn't about to let the change of coach get in the way of her plans.

All the boys from our class were there, as well as some from the class below. Kai-Tommy's father hooked up the ball with his hands. He had shiny black hair and was very slim for a dad. Then he started talking.

"We're going to have certain expectations of each one of you now. Next year, many of you will start playing in town, and if you want to make your mark, we're going to have to start thinking long-term. That means practicing three times a week, and nobody gets to stay home without a good reason."

I gulped.

"Gulliver, Halvor's dad, will be the assistant coach. He'll take care of the practical side of things. So if you've got any questions . . ."

Lena and I exchanged glances. Kai-Tommy's dad *and* Halvor's dad? This was some kind of plot!

"Who normally plays in goal?"

My jaw dropped. How could he possibly not know? Everybody in the area knew that Lena was the goalie on our team. She stepped into the circle wearing her goalkeeper's gloves and looked up defiantly at the man in the black tracksuit.

"Me."

"Just you?"

The others shuffled nervously, and then Halvor stepped into the circle.

"I used to stand in goal sometimes, and when Lena's out sick . . ." He quickly glanced at her, almost as if he was slightly scared.

Halvor, our new assistant coach's son and Kai-Tommy's best friend, must have grown about eight inches over the summer. His long arms hung down on each side, goalkeeper-like. Lena had grown a bit too, but she was just as skinny as before. And her mom couldn't be further from being an assistant coach. I'm not sure Ylva even knows the rules of the game.

I wonder if it was at that moment, standing in the circle with Halvor, that Lena realized things were going to change.

I don't want to remember the rest of that practice session. We had to run until our mouths tasted of blood, and I ended up last in almost all the drills. Never had I felt so out of place. Both Lena and Halvor were being tried out in goal, but I wasn't paying attention.

By the time we went home, Lena had scrapes on both her elbows and gravel on her face, and she was so tired that she got off her bike for the last hill. She didn't say a word until we were about to go our separate ways to our own houses. Then she looked out across the fjord and at Grandpa moseying up from by the old boat sheds.

"Don't stop coming, Trille."

I couldn't even answer her. The only thing I was thinking about was getting out of my wretched soccer clothes and into the shower.

"See you tomorrow," was all I said.

Then off I went.

CHAPTER TWELVE

The Salt Lick

*L*ena didn't ask about soccer again. She went alone to the next practice. I stood at the window and watched her cycle off without looking back. For two seconds, I felt like scrambling after her, but then I remembered about Kai-Tommy's dad and shuddered. I couldn't go through that again.

"Have you stopped playing soccer?" Dad asked.

I squirmed. I didn't really want to say I'd stopped. All the boys around here play soccer, after all.

"I'm taking a break," I mumbled.

Dad isn't usually one to let me avoid doing things.

But that day it was as if his thoughts were somewhere else.

"Well, if you're not going to soccer practice, you
can keep fit by lending your father a hand," he
said. "I was going to take up a new salt lick for the
sheep."

Was he joking? Our salt licks are twenty-two-
pound blocks of salt that give the sheep all sorts
of minerals they need, but this one had to go all
the way up to the Cliff. It would take the whole
afternoon. I was about to say something about child
labor, like Lena usually does, but then I saw the
furrow in his brow. Mom was lying asleep on the
sofa, and the kitchen looked like a disaster zone.

"OK," I said, heading out to the barn.

The Cliff is at the end of an endless mountain slope
that starts down by the sea and is steep all the way
up. I was breathing heavily long before I came close
to Hilltop Jon's farm. But then it was as if I found
my second wind. What if Birgit was home when
I went past?

Hillside had been in a pretty bad state the last

91

few years that Hilltop Jon and his horse, Molly, lived there. Tiles were missing from the roof of the barn, the paint was flaking off the walls, and there were clumps of long grass sticking out of all the berry plants. Now I narrowed my eyes as I stopped for a moment. The infield was green and freshly mown. Herbs and vegetables were growing in a row of planters. The roof of the barn was as leakproof as a rain jacket, and the walls were newly painted.

A smell of freshly baked bread came drifting out of the kitchen window. It hardly looked like the sort of disaster zone I was used to at home, I thought with dismay.

"Hi!" Birgit's father, the author, climbed down from a ladder on the far side of the house. "Trille, isn't it?"

I nodded, and then suddenly remembered that this man must hold me responsible for almost drowning his daughter.

"Are you looking for Birgit?"

I blushed and shook my head. I felt it was impossible to explain all about the salt lick in

English, so I just patted the bag and said, "For the sheep."

And then I sped off.

The track was slippery after all the rain of the past few days, but as long as I stepped on the rocks, it was fine. Small birch branches and alder twigs smacked me in the face. Dad should have been up here ages ago to clear the track with his clippers. Why hadn't he done it this year? All my life, I'd thought that parents could do anything. But now I was starting to doubt it. Things were in a complete state at home. It was all wrinkles and mess and sleeping and arguing.

I clenched my teeth and tried to think about nice things, but the salt lick rubbed hard against my back, and the hill was making my thighs ache.

"Trille?"

"Aaaah!"

Birgit and Haas suddenly appeared ahead of me.

"Going up the mountain?" she asked.

I nodded.

"Mushrooms," said Birgit, opening a large basket.

A yellow glow came from inside.

Wasn't it lethal to eat mushrooms? That's what I'd learned ever since I was little. You could die or get kidney stones just from swallowing a tiny piece of the wrong sort.

I don't exactly know how it happened, but Birgit put down her basket and came up the mountain with me. The warm September sun shone down on us, the track became drier, and the salt lick felt lighter. Neither of us said very much. She'd clearly been up there before. There's a visitors' book tucked into the small cairn that Minda and Dad made at the top, and her name was written there several times. Now she wanted to know the names of everything we could see. I strung up the salt lick and flopped myself down at the resting place by the cairn. Dad always points out places and tells me about them when we're up there. Oh, shear my sheep, if only I'd paid more attention! I told Birgit the names of the islands and mountains I was sure about.

"And that small one, all the way out there," I said

finally, "that's Kobbholmen. My grandmother lived there when she was little."

That made an impression on Birgit. Imagine having a grandmother who came from the sea. Grandpa was on his way out with *Troll*, probably going to set a net. Birgit looked at the tiny dot of a boat and wondered how I knew it was him.

I shrugged. "Is it true there aren't many hills in the Netherlands?"

It was. But there were other beautiful things. As the sun played cat and mouse with the clouds, Birgit told me in a mixture of English and Norwegian about her life there and the friends she'd left behind.

"Do you miss it?" I asked boldly.

She shrugged and smiled. She was used to missing places, she explained. "We travel so much."

Haas was lying down by my feet, looking at me curiously now and then.

"He's wondering where Lena is," Birgit said, laughing.

The dog opened his eyes wide when we mentioned her name. Lena takes chickens tobogganing, rides cattle, says "boo" to horses, and puts kittens in the dirty laundry to scare her mother. And yet I don't know of a single animal that doesn't like her.

"Lena's at soccer practice," I mumbled, gulping down my guilty conscience.

And she really had been practicing. She'd trained so hard that she was still completely furious when I popped in to see her later that evening.

"I hate gravel fields," she roared.

She was sitting on the kitchen table. She'd had a shower and was fiery red. Isak was cleaning the cuts on her knees and listening patiently to her as she shouted.

"Why can't we get an artificial-grass field in this stupid place, like everybody else has? Ow!"

I sat down on a chair and asked her tentatively how it had gone.

Lena snarled. "I hate boys, I hate coaches, and I hate gravel. What have you been up to, then?"

I told her about the salt lick, but I couldn't bring myself to tell her all the rest. That I'd been for a walk with Birgit, that I'd been invited into her house afterward and eaten fried chanterelle mushrooms on sourdough bread. That it was the best thing I'd tasted in all my life. And that I was slightly scared of dying of kidney failure, but it would almost have been worth it.

CHAPTER THIRTEEN

The Girls of the Class

*Y*ou're each going to choose a book," Ellisiv said as she looked at us. "And then you're going to give a presentation on the book and the author."

I felt a weight like a stone in my stomach. Speaking in front of the class is my worst nightmare.

"What's a gifted child like you got to worry about?" Lena usually says when I tell her about my fear.

It was Auntie Granny who always called me that. "You're such a gifted child, Trille," she used to say. "You'll go far." Lena thinks it's an excellent expression.

Nobody in the world has ever called Lena a gifted

child. She's good at PE and recess. If you ask her, everything else at school's a pain in the neck. Math is the worst. She and Andreas spend half of our math lessons out in a group study room with their own teacher. Lena's tried to explain to both Ylva and Ellisiv that it's pointless to get somebody to try to teach her math like that. She's going to be a goalie and will never have any need for all those sums. But it's no use. Ylva and Ellisiv are dead set on Lena learning math, just like every other person. I don't understand why they worry. Lena will manage fine.

I laid my head down heavily on the desk and stared at my wet sneakers.

"You're going to work in groups," I heard Ellisiv say, and I squeezed my eyes tightly shut. If I had to work with Kai-Tommy or Halvor, I might as well run away to sea.

"Trille, Lena, and Birgit. You can go and sit in the library . . ."

My heart skipped a whole stack of beats. I gathered my books up all in a fluster.

"Look, there go the three girls of the class," Kai-Tommy muttered as I passed.

Halvor and a few others snickered, but I pretended not to hear them. They weren't the ones getting to be in a group with Birgit.

Our library isn't big. I often go in the evenings with Mom, and I've read most of what they've got. Now Lena lay down on the sofa there, banging the heels of her wellies together with such force that the noise filled the whole room. Birgit and I each sat on a chair and put our notebooks on the table. The three of us had hardly been alone together since the raft-wreck.

"Let's pick *Emil and the Great Escape*," Lena said. She'd clearly made up her mind already. "I've got the movie of that one."

"Um, isn't it a bit childish?" I said with a cough.

"No. It's pretty short too," said Lena.

I looked at Birgit. She rarely said very much in class, but she seemed a bit more relaxed now.

"Sure, let's pick that one," she said.

She'd read the book in Dutch when she was younger. It would be a good way to improve her Norwegian, since she already knew the story. Besides, she'd learned about Astrid Lindgren, the author, for a school project a few years ago, and we thought we could include a bit about her other books too.

"Fine by me," said Lena. "But I want to do the bit about *Emil and the Great Escape*—"

"Because you've got the movie," I said, finishing her sentence for her.

On weekdays, Lena and I are always the first ones home. When we get there, we rummage through all the cupboards in both our houses for something to keep us alive until dinner. Dad's started hiding his favorite cookies in the sock drawer in his bedroom. On that particular day, there was a fruit bowl with some old grapes in our kitchen, so we sat down there.

"What a mess," Lena sighed, tidying up the newspapers on the table so she could get to the tablet lying underneath. "Are things completely out of control here?"

I looked around. It really was pretty chaotic in our house at the moment.

"Do you all expect Kari to go around like a

garbage collector, tidying up after you? In the middle of The Change? It's not easy, you know. I asked Isak."

I was about to remind Lena that I'd carried a massive salt lick all the way up to the Cliff the day before, but instead I opened the dishwasher and started emptying it. Birgit was going to come down when she'd had something to eat. The house couldn't look like this then!

"Smoking haddocks, we should make a movie about *Emil and the Great Escape*," said Lena. "Ellisiv would be blown away. Then you wouldn't have to speak, Trille."

She said it in a perfectly normal way, as if it were the most natural thing in the world that standing in front of the whole class made me panic. I wrung out the cloth that was in the sink. It smelled foul.

"Did you know this?" Lena asked. She was using the tablet, swiping her fingers eagerly across the screen. "In the seventies, there was a TV series of *Emil*, but they didn't show the whole thing here in Norway. They were scared that children would start hoisting each other up flagpoles, like Emil does with his little sister, Ida."

She munched the old grapes as she read on. "What a load of rubbish! We've got to have that in our presentation. Actually, how about we . . ."

I pictured little Ida at the top of the flagpole. Sometimes I just know what Lena's thinking.

"Who are you planning to hoist up?" I asked, chucking the stinky cloth in with the laundry.

Lena closed the cover on the tablet.

"It will have to be whoever's lightest. Shall we go and pick up Krølla from her after-school program?"

CHAPTER FOURTEEN

Krølla at Half-Mast

Strictly speaking, we should have waited until
Birgit arrived to start our book project, but
we had to get this particular scene filmed while our
parents were still at work. That much was clear even
to me. I quickly fetched my bike, and we sped off to
school. Krølla hates her after-school program. Every
day she asks Mom if she can go home with Lena and
me instead. For some reason or other, Mom thinks
that's completely out of the question.

It wasn't hard to persuade Krølla to be part of Lena's
film stunt. Before we knew it, she'd gone and found

her red dress, so she would look like little Ida.

"You'll end up in two pieces if we tie that thing around your waist," Lena said, peering at the thin cord on the flagpole. "We'll need to use Magnus's climbing harness."

It was probably around then that I realized this was a bad idea. Magnus's property is sacred, but Lena's never worried about that.

"He never uses it anyway!" she said.

The harness was far too big for Krølla, so Lena immediately adjusted every single strap. My brother was going to go berserk, but at least Krølla was secure in the harness. Lena fixed her to the flagpole rope with a carabiner.

"We have to get this done before Magnus comes home," I said. "Are you all right, Krølla?"

She put on her sunglasses and gave a thumbs-up.

"Take one. Action!" Lena shouted from over on the lawn, filming with her cell phone camera.

That Emil must have been strong! It was hard work hoisting Krølla. I sent a thought to the top of the flagpole, hoping that the hole the rope went through could bear the load. With every pull, Krølla came closer to the sky. She clucked away happily up there. I was struggling and sweating, but trying my best to stay cool. This video was going to be shown to the whole class, after all!

Krølla was only a couple of yards from the top when somebody coughed behind us.

It was Birgit and Haas. Why did she always suddenly appear like that? I gave such a start I lost my grip for a brief second. Krølla slid down the flagpole with a wail, Haas barked, and Birgit put her hand to her mouth. Miraculously, Krølla came to a stop just over halfway up the pole.

"Are you all right?" I shouted, trembling.

"I'm stuck!"

Lena looked accusingly at Birgit. "We were in the middle of filming a scene here!"

"Sorry," Birgit whispered.

The problem now was that we couldn't get Krølla up or down. She'd gotten herself stuck on a hook. No matter how much we jiggled and tugged, she wouldn't budge.

"Perfect," I sighed, as I saw the school bus stopping up the road.

The high school students were glued to the bus windows, examining the scene in our garden. I could see from Minda's face a hundred yards away that she was mortified.

"What's wrong with you?" she snarled furiously as she threw down her bag.

"I can see all the way to Mariannelund!" Krølla shouted bravely, trying to quote from the story about Emil and Ida.

Then Magnus saw the harness. "Seriously?"

"We're only borrowing it," Lena said calmly. "Safety's our top priority."

Magnus was about to blow his top, but Minda stopped him. "Can't you for once try thinking about other people instead of yourself and your stupid stuff? We've got to get her down!"

My brother and sister tried jiggling the cord too, but Krølla was truly stuck, strung up there like a dried fish in the north wind. Magnus went to fetch a ladder, and just as he came back with it, the door to the basement apartment opened and out came

Grandpa. He's always having an afternoon nap when we come home from school. Now he screwed up his eyes as he looked at each one of us and then up at the flagpole. He was holding the telephone.

"Vera Johansen just phoned to see if I was dead."

"Huh?" I blurted out.

Grandpa scratched his chin drowsily. "Yes, since our flag was flying at half-mast," he explained. "So I told her I was only having a nap, which I was."

I glanced nervously at Birgit. If she didn't already think we were completely off our rockers, she certainly would now. Why couldn't we just for once have a normal afternoon in the cove?

The ladder was no use — it was too unstable. Grandpa thought we'd have to use the tractor bucket to lift somebody up. Krølla sighed. She was starting to get bored now.

Mom came home from work at the worst moment imaginable. Grandpa was driving the tractor and concentrating on getting the bucket the right distance from the flagpole, while Minda was doing the best she could to cling on inside the bucket. Magnus was hanging on to the side of the tractor, giving directions. On the ground, a terrified girl from the Netherlands was trying to calm her barking dog, while Lena was standing on the table in the yard, wearing the world's largest grin as she filmed the whole scene from the perfect angle. I was holding the flag rope tightly, hoping that my little sister dangling up there was enough of a dramatic sight to stop Mom from noticing the deep ditches dug by the tractor tires right across the flower bed and half the lawn.

"What in heaven's name is going on here?" Mom shouted.

"Trille and Lena have to do a book presentation," Magnus explained.

And Krølla's never going to be allowed to stop going to her after-school program, I thought to myself.

CHAPTER FIFTEEN

Mom Goes to the Doctor

It was that afternoon I decided to have a chat with Mom. Secretly, I'd been keeping an eye on her for several weeks to see if Lena's theory about The Change was true. After all, how could Lena be so sure that's what it was? What if it was something else? Mothers can get ill. My own grandmother had died young. She had been a mother too, just as much as my mom. It's not right for things like that to happen. Every time I thought about it, it was almost as if I couldn't breathe. The more I kept an eye out, the more worried I felt. Was Mom a bit fatter? She had more gray hair now, anyway, and she slept and slept, night and day.

There was nobody I could ask either. Dad had wrinkles on his brow and was getting worked up about the slightest things, while Minda just interrupted me in an annoyed way if I tried to ask her. Plus I couldn't bring myself to talk to Grandpa about it. What would he know about menopause?

But that day, when Mom started crying just because Krølla was hanging from a flagpole, unharmed and perfectly fine, I couldn't leave it any longer.

So when evening came and everything had calmed down, I made some warm cocoa for her and sat down next to where she was lying on the sofa.

"Oh, thank you, Trille!" she said, clearly surprised, and sat up.

There had been a bit of bedlam and commotion after the business with the flagpole, but now the house was quiet.

"Mom. Don't you think you should go to the doctor to get your menopause checked out?"

"What?"

I wished Lena were there to explain, but she wasn't.

"Well, your body's changing, and you're getting a bit fat and fed up," I said glumly. "And it's probably just the menopause, but—"

Mom choked on her cocoa, sending it splattering halfway across the living-room table.

"Fat?" she shouted.

I gulped. "Well, maybe not exactly fat, but . . ."

Mom looked at me. "What is it, Trille?"

I poked at the sofa cushion. "What if it's something dangerous? What if you have cancer?" I eventually said under my breath.

"Are you worried about that?"

All I could do was nod, as there was a lump in my throat now.

"Oh, Trille!" Mom stroked my hair. "I'll be turning forty-five next spring. I'm not young anymore."

Wasn't she trying to make me feel better? Saying that she was old didn't help! Old people get cancer all the time.

"I haven't got as much energy as I used to. So maybe I feel a bit tired and cross when I've got a lot on my plate. And fat too."

She prodded one of the bulges on her stomach.

"Just a bit softer," I lied.

Mom snorted with laughter. "But that's the way it is with menopause. It's nothing serious."

I thought about all her sleeping and bossiness. Was it really nothing bad?

"Would you feel better about it if I went to the doctor to see if everything's all right?" Mom asked eventually.

I nodded.

"Then that's what I'll do first thing tomorrow, my darling Trille. Now, go and fetch some buns from the freezer, and we'll make ourselves even softer."

I felt as light as a feather that evening. I should have told Mom before that I was worried about her. She was only too happy to talk about it!

But the next afternoon, everything was as bad as it had been before. Mom's face looked all strange, and she asked the whole family to sit around the kitchen table.

"I've been to see the doctor today," she said, picking at the tablecloth, as if she didn't know how to continue.

Dad stood over by the sink with an empty coffee mug, looking down at the floor. My heart was struggling to beat normally.

"Have you got cancer?" I whispered.

Minda and Magnus stared at me in shock.

"Huh? Cancer?"

"No, no, no," said Mom. "I haven't got cancer. And it's not menopause either."

Dad made a strange sniffling noise over by the sink. Mom turned toward him. Then she started sniffling too, and suddenly they broke down and started laughing so hard the whole kitchen echoed. They looked at each other, gasping for air as they laughed and laughed and laughed.

Minda, Magnus, Krølla, and I sat motionless on our chairs. Our parents had gone completely bonkers. Who was going to look after us now? Grandpa?

"Mom . . ." I squeaked.

Then Mom pulled herself together and shouted: "You're going to have a brother!" She poked a finger at her soft tummy. "For Christmas. No wonder I'm fat! He's been in there almost five months!"

"WHAT?" Magnus shouted. "You're kidding!"

"Oh, good grief," Minda mumbled. "Seriously? I didn't think old people like you could have babies." She put her head in her hands. "Mom, you're old enough to be a grandmother!" she moaned from under there.

Big brothers and sisters must be related to aliens. What was wrong with them? Couldn't they see that this was absolutely fantastic? Mom wasn't sick! And we were going to have a baby. I leaped up onto my chair.

"Yippee!" I shouted. "Yippee times a hundred and three!"

Krølla leaped up onto her chair too and threw her arms in the air. "Yippee times a hundred and two hundred!" she yelled.

"That's more like it," said Mom, looking sternly at Minda and Magnus.

Then they couldn't help smiling too. Still, Minda made sure to tell me it was so embarrassing, and that even a little kid like me should realize that.

"And Lena thought it was menopause!" I said, almost shouting, dashing out the door with the news.

But I stopped midway between our houses. Lena

was only going to be partially pleased about this. She'd been asking for a little brother loudly enough to make the walls tremble over there, and so far it had all been in vain. Meanwhile, at our place, the whole Change situation had transformed into a baby.

I turned back. I had to have a little think about how I was going to tell her. People should be happy when they hear news like that.

I could have spared myself the thought. Krølla went over and spilled the beans later that evening. Ylva's teaching her to knit, and while they're knitting, Krølla blabbers on about anything and everything.

When darkness fell, Lena came crashing in. She had rain in her hair and thunder in her eyes.

"Is it true, Kari?"

Mom caught Lena in an enormous hug. "It's as true as the tide, Lena Lid."

Lena wriggled loose. "But it was our turn now, Kari!"

"You can borrow him whenever you want, Lena."

"Borrow him? Is this some kind of library you're running?"

Lena wondered if we had the faintest drop of an idea what it was like wishing for a brother as intensely as she did while children just came shooting out of the house next door.

"I understand, Lena," said Mom.

Lena doubted it. "Have you ever counted your children, Kari? We've only got me at my place! Only me!"

Mom assured her that she counted us every evening, especially now that Minda and Magnus were capable of staying out until late at night.

"But Reidar and I spent many long years together before we became parents. Not everybody can have children, and it often takes much longer than you'd like."

I looked up, astonished. Had Mom and Dad once been childless? What did they do back then?

Lena looked skeptically at Mom. "Anyway, you should leave giving birth to younger people, Kari. You've got gray hair."

Mom agreed about that last bit. But she couldn't be anything other than happy at that moment.

CHAPTER SIXTEEN

Drama in the
Lid Family Kitchen

*T*he next afternoon, I popped down to see
Grandpa.

"Five times a grandfather soon!" I said, smiling.

"That's right. It's great stuff, Trille. Great stuff.
Hey, look at this."

He passed me a picture across the kitchen table.

"I found it when I was sorting out my writing
desk. Do you remember it?"

I nodded. It was the one of the huge halibut. I'd
seen it many times before. I leaned over and studied
it again. Grandpa was young and had blond hair, like
me. He was leaning proudly against the wall of the

boat shed. Next to him hung the enormous fish.

"Were you alone when you caught it?" I asked.

"No, I wasn't. Inger was with me. In fact I doubt I'd have landed that halibut on my own."

It was probably my grandmother who'd taken the picture, I thought, trying to imagine it like a movie.

"Look here," said Grandpa, pushing another picture across the table.

I hadn't seen this one before. "Where is it?"

"On the dock in Baltimore."

I stared at the photo. Grandpa in the United States. He looked cool, sitting there with his pipe in his mouth and his sleeves rolled up.

"I sailed abroad for a couple of years before I got married."

"That must've been exciting," I said.

"It was." He took back the picture and looked at it. Then he shook his head a little. "I was so blooming homesick."

"Were you?"

"I was. Inger was around then, you see."

"Have you got a picture of her too?" I asked.

"Mmm . . . yes."

Grandpa went over to his desk and came back with a small bundle of photos. I'd seen them before, but that was a long time ago. There was one of Inger, Dad, and Uncle Tor out on the steps, and one of Inger wearing an apron in a kitchen full of fish. But the best one was of Granny on her own on board *Troll*. She was wearing a big pair of waterproof overalls, her hair was standing straight up, and her mouth was open, laughing.

"What was she really like?" I asked.

"Heh," said Grandpa, resting his chin on his hand. He looked briefly at me and then at the pictures. "Well, it was Inger or nobody, put it that way."

Then he held up the picture from Baltimore again.

"I'd made a real mess of things before I left, Trille. The whole love story could just as easily have gone to pot, I'll tell you that."

"What happened?"

He gathered up the pictures. "Well, wouldn't you like to know!" He put the pictures back in the desk drawer.

"But was it all right in the end?" I asked.

"Everything turns out all right for good-looking

men like us," Grandpa said, shutting the drawer with a bang. "Shall we take an evening stroll to the boat shed?"

"I've got to go and see Lena. We're doing a book project."

Grandpa stuffed his hands in his pockets. "Just let me know when you've got time for a trip out on the boat, then. It's a long time since we last went out."

I promised I would, and ran off.

There was a gloomy atmosphere in the Lid kitchen. Ylva and Lena were doing math homework.

"Congratulations on your good news," said Ylva, smiling tiredly.

I thanked her and sat down at the table.

"Kari's very happy," said Lena. "She's very happy with all her children."

"Mm-hmm," said Ylva, straightening her glasses so she could read the math question again.

"Were you very happy when you had me?" Lena asked.

"Mm-hmm," said Ylva again, moving her finger down along the page.

Sometimes I think the house could collapse around Ylva without her noticing. Now Lena took the math book and pushed it away across the table.

"Were you very happy when you had me, even though you had to stop going to school and Dad ran off?" she shouted.

For as long as I've known Lena, I've been able to tell when a storm is brewing. This time it was completely unexpected. Lena swung out an arm, flinging her math book to the floor with considerable force, and started to march out.

"What kind of a question is that?" Ylva shouted.

Lena was about to shout something back, but instead she just threw out her arms, as if she couldn't be bothered explaining.

And then the shock came. Ylva took off her glasses and said, "No. I wasn't very happy."

Complete silence fell over the Lid kitchen.

"Huh?" said Lena over by the door.

"I was far too young. I was playing in a band and was halfway through a school year. Plus your dad didn't want to be a dad. I wasn't happy. I was terrified."

I'd never heard the clock ticking in Lena's kitchen before. Now it sounded like it was slicing through the air.

"You know that the first few years were difficult, Lena."

Not a sound.

"But," said Ylva, "I didn't know it was possible to care about someone as much as I care about you, either."

Lena drew a breath, and Ylva put on her glasses.

"Just tell me if you know of a mother who loves her little girl more than I do," she said, picking up the math book.

I could see that Lena was thinking very hard, but luckily nobody came to mind. She came and sat back down at the table.

"Are you going to make me a little brother sometime soon, then?"

"Oh, good grief," Ylva moaned. "Let Trille take over. I'm going to do some knitting with Krølla."

* * *

When Birgit arrived, first she gazed in awe at all of the colorful art everywhere, like most people do when they come into Lena's house, and then she smiled at us as if she was really looking forward to working on our group project. She'd brought along a big bottle of homemade bilberry squash.

Ylva uses a lot of film in her art projects, and now she'd taught Lena how to use one of her editing programs on the computer. In the office corner under the attic stairs, Lena showed us the video from the yard on the big monitor. I thought it was embarrassing to see myself, but Birgit laughed.

"This is going to be fabulous!" she said.

Lena wanted to add some music and captions. Birgit and I sat down at the kitchen table to plan the rest. I'd never worked with anybody like Birgit before. She didn't sit there complaining about being bored: quite the opposite. She talked and explained things and made everything seem easy and fun. She told me she was slightly dreading speaking Norwegian in front of the class, but she thought it would be all right as long as she wrote down what she wanted to say.

"Maybe you could tell them about the book, and I could talk about the author?" she suggested.

"Mm-hmm," I said, trying to smile while my stomach tied itself in knots.

Lena looked at me over the top of the computer screen and frowned.

Then Isak came home from work.

"Do we need any popcorn here?" he asked as he put his bag down in the hallway.

What could we do but say yes to a question like that? Soon he'd made us some in a big pot.

"Thanks, Dad," Lena said quickly as he went off into the living room.

She blushed when she saw that I'd heard her and plonked the bowl of popcorn down with a thud on top of one of my books.

We'd just finished eating when the doorbell rang.

"Not a moment's peace," Lena sighed, heading out into the hallway.

On the doorstep, she found Kai-Tommy and Halvor.

"Yes?" Lena's voice was quizzical, as if she were speaking to two senile men who had wandered off from the retirement home.

Kai-Tommy swept back his hair. "Is Birgit here?"

We couldn't exactly hide Birgit in the fridge and say no. Soon the two boys were sitting at the kitchen table too, looking in astonishment at everything around them.

"Your mom said you were here," Kai-Tommy explained to Birgit.

Birgit smiled. Couldn't she see what an insane situation this was? I thought about all the horrible things Kai-Tommy had said and done to Lena over the years. And about the things he'd said to me. Birgit had no idea of all that. It was almost as if she'd landed from space straight into our class. Was it really possible that Kai-Tommy could seem like a nice person if you didn't already know him?

"We had some popcorn, but I'm sorry to say we've run out," Lena said, although that "sorry" didn't sound particularly convincing.

Halvor and I didn't say a word. But Kai-Tommy

poured himself a glass of bilberry squash and acted as if he'd always been a frequent guest at Lena's house. I was disheartened to realize that he was probably going to be just as tall and dark-haired as his father.

"Birgit, do you want to come and see the game tomorrow?" he suddenly asked. "We're playing against the team from the islands. Our first game since the summer."

I was about to reply that Birgit wasn't interested in soccer when she said that she'd be happy to go.

"Will you be playing too?" she asked Lena.

Lena glanced quickly at Halvor and nodded. I felt totally left out. Soggy shepherds, I'd been planning on carrying up a salt lick instead. Or going for a trip out to sea, or doing something else meaningful. Blasted soccer.

"Are you going to come, Trille?" Birgit asked.

I coughed. It would be really embarrassing to turn up to watch when I'd been part of the team until just recently. But I imagined sitting next to Birgit in the stands. That would be quite something.

If she was impressed by Kai-Tommy's hard shots, I could just tell her that he had poor technical abilities. I agreed to go, very reluctantly.

When I was about to leave, Lena stopped me by the door.

"Will we be all right doing that presentation, then?"

I looked at the doorbell and bit the inside of my cheek.

"Of course."

CHAPTER SEVENTEEN

Game-Day Madness

*H*i, Trille. Are you injured?"

Axel, our old coach, plopped himself down next to me in the ramshackle soccer stands.

"Sort of," I mumbled. "What about you?"

"No, I'm training the younger ones now," Axel said cheerily. "Ivar wanted to take on your team. He's pretty good, you know."

I was about to protest, but then I spotted Birgit. She parked her bike over by the mini-field, where she met Ellisiv, who had probably been working. They walked together across the school playground. When Birgit spotted me, she waved, and a rocket burst inside my chest.

"Have you got a girlfriend?" Axel asked, nudging me.

"Um, no." I could feel myself blushing all the way to my earlobes. "What about you? Are you spending a lot of time at the café these days?"

Axel laughed as he made space for Ellisiv and Birgit.

"My girlfriend dumped me, Trille. So I don't have to go to the café anymore."

"She dumped you?"

"Like a sack of potatoes. Hi, Ellisiv."

So we sat there, Axel and I, both of us next to a girl who wasn't our girlfriend, watching the game. It was incredible. Birgit asked me questions the whole time, and every so often she laughed her soft, pretty laugh. It was wonderful not playing soccer anymore. Lena was right. You can't keep on doing things you hate.

And as if to make things even better, Kai-Tommy missed the goal by miles a couple of times and shouted nasty words across the field. I hoped Birgit had noticed that. But it didn't look like she cared. Maybe she didn't know enough Norwegian yet.

The warm sun shone down on us, and it would all have been perfect if it hadn't been for one thing spoiling the mood: in goal, where once there had stood a skinny girl shouting herself hoarse, there now stood Halvor, strapping and silent. The more time that passed, the more uncomfortable I felt. Was Ivar going to bring Lena on at all?

"Is Lena injured too?" Axel asked.

I shook my head and tried to push aside the bad feeling I had seeing her sitting down alone on the bench. None of the boys were sitting there.

She wasn't brought on after halftime either. Not even when Halvor let in a real howler of a goal. Eventually we were down three to nil. Ivar shouted and gave the boys instructions without losing his temper. It didn't look like he cared what the result was. The boys on the field were struggling.

"But why isn't Lena playing?" Ellisiv asked.

Axel said something about how it was a good idea to have two goalies, and that they probably wanted to let Halvor gain some confidence between the goalposts, in case Lena got injured. I gulped. I wasn't having a good time anymore, no matter how nice it was to be sitting next to Birgit. My neighbor was sitting down there on the substitutes' bench, with her cap low over her face, her goalkeeper's gloves on, and a dark cloud above her.

Lena was brought on five minutes before the end. A shot came on target, which she easily saved, and then the game was finished.

I found Lena at home down by the barn. She was kicking a ball against the wall. The seagulls jumped into the sky with every shot.

"Halvor's got to have a turn too, so it wouldn't be a total disaster if you got injured," I said cautiously.

Lena stopped shooting the ball and looked at me as if I were the stupidest person in God's creation.

"Disaster? We lost the game! I'm better than him, Trille!"

Another crash against the barn.

"But —" I began.

"Halvor's in goal because his dad's the assistant coach!"

Lena gave the ball one last mad kick, sending it flying all the way down to the beach. The barn breathed a sigh of relief through the gap in the wall.

"What are you going to do about it, then?" I asked, feeling a bit worn out by her always getting angry about everything.

"I suppose I'll have to become a boy," she muttered furiously, heading off without even picking up her gloves.

CHAPTER EIGHTEEN

Keisha

*Y*ou used to live in Africa?"

I looked around Birgit's room in amazement. The last time I visited her I'd only been in the kitchen. Today we were finishing our book presentation. Lena was at soccer practice and was going to join us later.

I gazed at all the pictures of giraffes and elephants. On Birgit's desk was a picture of her with summer hair almost as white as chalk. She had her arm around a girl who was as dark as Birgit was fair.

"Mom and some other people started a coffee roastery in Amsterdam," Birgit said, going on to explain that the coffee beans came from small farms in Kenya. "We spent a year living there while she was arranging everything."

The very thought of all she'd experienced made me feel light-headed.

"Why didn't you say you'd lived in Kenya?" I asked, bewildered, remembering how Lena had gone on and on about a measly vacation to Crete.

Birgit shrugged. "I don't know. I haven't met many other people who've been to Kenya, so it feels a bit weird to talk about it, I suppose."

I stared in fascination at the picture on her desk. Birgit looked so happy in it.

"That's Keisha," she said. "I miss her a lot. But we chat online."

"I'd like to hear more about Kenya," I said.

"OK," Birgit replied happily, pulling out a big photo album from her shelf.

We sat down on her bed, and she showed me pictures and told me about them. Her words took me to a green and warm place that smelled of coffee. She told me about rainy mornings, about the big animals, and about the house they'd lived in. But most of all she told me about Keisha, the best friend in the world.

"We've decided that we'll go and study together one day," she said. "Maybe you'd like to come too?"

I suddenly felt all warm. "Mm-hmm," I nodded.

Study? I always thought I would stay in Mathildewick Cove until my dying day. I even had my eye on a piece of land down by the sea where I would build my house. And then I'd imagined that I would be a fisherman, like Grandpa. Now it was as if the world had opened up in all directions. Could people just travel around and do whatever they wanted? Could I do that too?

Then Birgit put away the album. We had to get to work. We'd finished writing the presentation, and that evening we just had to practice in front of each other. Birgit and I took turns standing by the computer and talking. I spoke about Emil, and she spoke about the author, Astrid Lindgren, in her own beautiful kind of Norwegian. When we'd done it twice each, Lena sent a message to say she wasn't coming. I pictured her sitting in the usual spot on the kitchen table, getting bandaged up again. Had practice been as awful as the game the day before?

"That's all right," said Birgit. "We're finished anyway. I'm a bit nervous about it, you know."

I nodded and felt a little as if I couldn't breathe properly.

Before I left, Birgit's mom asked if I'd stay to have something to eat with them. She served up a hot, bright-red soup that tasted pretty strong. Did they always eat dinner that late? We all sat around the table, just like at home. Birgit's parents asked me about the farm and fishing and the mountains as if I were a grown-up. They wanted to hear about all the things I thought were ordinary and boring. I did my best to explain in a mixture of English and Norwegian, but it was difficult.

I felt completely dizzy as I walked home. My head was bursting with new thoughts, and my stomach was full of new food. When I went to bed, I lay there, staring at the ceiling. What was I going to do? There was no way I could let Birgit find out I was too scared even to stand up in front of my own class. I couldn't go to school the next day. I couldn't face it.

Lena was the only person who knew I wasn't

really ill, but she didn't say a word about it. She just gave me that raised-eyebrow look she'd started doing, and then told me about the book presentation when she came home. It had been a smash hit, according to her. People had, of course, long since heard about the flagpole incident, so it was a real highlight for the class to get to see it with their own eyes.

"You made a good impression, Trille," she assured me.

The next day, Birgit seemed worried when she asked me if I felt better. I nodded and looked away. Did she realize what a little wimp I was?

CHAPTER NINETEEN

The Ruler Stunt That Went Wrong

I was thinking more and more about Birgit. It was almost as if a gentle and gracious bird had landed in the middle of our class and was able to see beyond all the stupidity and daftness. For example, one day we were working in pairs, and Birgit was with Andreas. In the first few years at school, Kai-Tommy used to mimic Andreas every time he opened his mouth, because he stammers. When we got Ellisiv as our teacher, the bullying stopped, but it was already too late. Andreas hardly ever said another word. But the day he worked with Birgit, I was surprised to hear him chatting away. In another lesson, she might chat the same way with Kai-Tommy, as if he were a totally normal and pleasant person. Was that what he was like when he was with Birgit?

I was crestfallen every time I saw the two of them together. He liked her; there was no doubt about that. And I was nothing compared to Kai-Tommy.

I soon became an expert at finding ways to spend time with Birgit outside of school. Dad was stunned by how many salt licks I was willing to carry up the mountain, and when the sheep had been brought down for the winter, I went up with the hedge clippers instead. Birgit liked being up the mountain and thought doing the trimming along the track was great fun. The same went for her Norwegian homework: she often needed help with it, and Kai-Tommy certainly didn't have anything to offer there. A gifted child like me, on the other hand, could teach her all about grammar and sentence construction until the sheep came home, so to speak.

I didn't mean to spend less time at sea with Grandpa. That's just how things went. I didn't mean to spend less time with Lena either. That's just how things went too.

As autumn tightened its grip and I went gallivanting around Hillside with Birgit, Grandpa went out to sea alone. I would see him doing his usual rounds from the house to the boat shed, and from the boat shed to the pier. Some days I would run down to him, sit on a fish box, and have a little chat, but I never stayed for long. Grandpa didn't mention it. But sometimes I noticed he'd be looking for me after I'd gone.

As for Lena, she was fighting for her life on the soccer field. And she was all alone too. Our team played game after game, but she was only ever sent on to play for the last five minutes. She argued and got angry, but she kept going to every single practice. Three times a week she came home covered in gravel and scraped all over. I often popped through the hedge and over to the Lid family kitchen on those evenings. It was good for Lena to have somebody to shout at: that much was clear.

Usually Isak would be sitting there, patching her

up while the rage flew around him. I would pull up a chair too and listen with half an ear. But Ylva thought things had gone too far.

"Can't you just give up soccer?" she asked one evening when Lena was sitting again on what had become the official medical station, the kitchen table.

"Give it up?"

"All you do is moan about it, Lena. If it's that terrible, then aren't there other things that would be better?" Ylva tried suggesting.

"What would those be? Keyboard lessons?" Lena's voice was so sharp you could cut yourself on it.

Ylva replied that she hadn't said a word about keyboard lessons, but now that Lena mentioned it, it wouldn't hurt to practice a bit more.

"Or, to put it another way," she said, correcting herself, "it wouldn't hurt to do any practice at all." Then she continued, "Look at Trille."

I felt like I'd been caught red-handed. Not only had I started hovering around Hillside all the time, but I'd also started practicing the piano. I wouldn't admit it even at knifepoint, but I was only doing it to impress Birgit and her family. I didn't want to sound like an idiot at the music school's Christmas concert.

"You'll never be good at something if you don't practice," Ylva added.

After that, Lena stopped complaining. She kept going to soccer practice, looking like a shadow of her usual self, but she never said a word when she came home.

And then she broke her hand.

"How on earth can you break your hand in an English lesson?" Magnus wanted to know.

Lena explained that there was no telling what terrible things might happen if you were bored for long enough, and that our English lessons were so boring they'd been a risk to her health for some time now.

I was there when it happened. Lena was trying out one of her ruler stunts. She'd developed a technique that involved sticking a ruler into the wall like a sword, then tipping her chair in such a way that the ruler is the only thing holding her up. While Ellisiv was reading out a long text about the school day in Australia, I could see Lena was daring herself to tip

143

even farther back in her chair, until she was almost horizontal. The ruler quivered under the strain. It certainly looked impressive.

Lena was concentrating so hard that she didn't notice everybody, including Ellisiv, starting to peer in her direction. Then, just as the schoolchildren in Australia had gone home for the day and Ellisiv was about to say "Lena Lid" in the way only she can, we heard a sharp crack as the ruler broke, and a much louder crash as the chair slipped away and Lena slammed to the floor.

"Do you know what my mom said, Trille?" Lena grumbled the next day on the way to our music lessons.

"No."

"She said: 'What bad timing with the music school concert coming up.'"

Lena waved her plaster cast around in agitation. "Floundering flatfish, never mind about the concert!" she shouted. "Now I can't play in goal!"

I closed my ears. I couldn't stand to hear any more about soccer.

"Why are you going to your music lesson today, then?"

"To show Mr. Rognstad my plaster cast. He's going to be relieved, I bet."

I shuddered. The music school concert in December stood out like a dark spot on the calendar. It was exactly the same as with the book presentation. I'd have to do something in front of loads of people. But this time I wasn't going to chicken out. I couldn't. If I was ill again that day, then Birgit would work it out. So I was going to practice, practice, practice.

It was the only way to survive.

CHAPTER TWENTY

"Für Elise"

*A*nd practice I did. "Für Elise," the piece that had looked utterly impossible when I'd first seen the notes on paper, eventually turned into music. My improvement put Mr. Rognstad into a kind of positive state of shock. He didn't know that I was being driven by pure fear. I might sit by the piano wishing for a drum kit until my head ached, but still I gritted my teeth and got my fingers to sweep over all the right keys. I wanted to be able to play "Für Elise" in my sleep, with my eyes closed, and even if my mind went blank. It was the only way to get through the concert. Birgit and her family had to see that I could do more than build rafts and gut fish.

Every afternoon, I sat at the piano while Grandpa puttered around in the boat shed and Lena was down by the barn with one broken hand and a soccer ball. I could see her from the window. Sometimes she just did keepie-uppies, and other times she went down to Grandpa and fetched some fishing buoys, which she set out in the field. She'd drawn a line that was supposed to be the edge of the six-yard box. She put the ball down there, and then she aimed and took long goal kicks toward the fishing buoys.

That's how we went on all through November and half of December. Grandpa in the boat shed, Lena outside the barn, and me at the piano.

By the time the Christmas holidays and the music school concert were approaching, I could play "Für Elise" without so much as peeking at the notes. Grandpa had fixed and mended every single net he could find, and Lena's ball was slamming into the fishing buoys with ever-growing precision. She'd managed a dizzying 1,011 keepie-uppies in a row too. Strangely enough, she didn't boast about this to anybody—not even to the boys in our class. She'd stopped talking about soccer.

* * *

"I'll come and listen," Lena came to say through the window, the day before the concert. "I'll clap even if it's a complete racket."

"It's not going to be a complete racket," I said.

"No, but if it is. You've got to squeeze out the whole of 'Für Elise' on that thing."

In any case, she promised to drum her plaster cast on the back of the chair in front and whistle along. She also wanted to savor all the other performers' nerves. Especially Kai-Tommy's.

"Although . . . I almost hope it goes well for him."

"What?" I'd never heard Lena say anything nice about Kai-Tommy before, and deep down I didn't like it.

"Well, it's just . . . Ivar's not fair to him," Lena mumbled.

I thought she was going to start whining about her goalkeeping career again, but instead she said that the person who got yelled at the most at practice was Kai-Tommy.

"The other boys are just as bad, you know,

except perhaps Andreas. He's good at reading the game . . ."

She didn't say any more after that. It was as if she'd forgotten herself for a moment.

"Are you looking forward to Christmas?" she asked instead, resting her chin on the windowsill.

"Mm-hmm," I said. "What about you?"

"Yup. Birgit's going to the Netherlands, isn't she?"

I nodded. Why was Lena asking that? Was she pleased? She was smiling anyway.

"We're going to set a new record with our haul of sweets when we go caroling this year, Trille. Mark my words."

Then she pulled her head out of the window without so much as saying bye.

I started playing "Für Elise" again, even though Magnus had said that he was going to be hospitalized if I played that piece one more time. From the corner of my eye, I saw Lena crossing the frosty fields in the low December sunlight. She met Grandpa down by the boat shed. I wondered what they were talking about as they strolled out onto the breakwater together. Suddenly I felt such a longing to be down there with them, it was like something slicing through my chest. But I'd agreed with Birgit that I'd go up to Hillside so we could study for our Norwegian test.

CHAPTER TWENTY-ONE

The Christmas Present

*T*he music school concert was a blur. I can't even remember going up when it was my turn. But my plan worked. I knew "Für Elise" so well that I played it even though I was sitting on-stage like a dead monkey. In any case, Mom, with her huge tummy, said it had gone well. And Mr. Rognstad clapped, clearly pleased.

I came back to my senses when it was Kai-Tommy's turn. He started off well but then ground to a complete halt halfway through and had to start again. A nasty little feeling of satisfaction grew inside me. I glanced over at Lena. Her brows were knitted, and when Kai-Tommy finished, she burst into thunderous applause.

I tried to spot Birgit, but I couldn't see her slender frame until she took her seat onstage. People probably thought they were about to hear something ordinary and halfway decent, like when the rest of us played, but then Birgit started blazing away, playing something by Grieg that sent chills and waves of warmth down my spine.

There was total silence when she finished. Then the deafening applause began. I could see that Mom was extremely impressed. Only Lena seemed unenthusiastic, slapping her good hand half-heartedly against her thigh. She seriously doesn't have a clue about music.

Just as I was getting into Mom's car at the end, somebody grabbed on to my jacket.

"Here," said Birgit. "A Christmas present." She pushed a parcel into my lap.

"Oh, thank you!"

"I'll see you in the new year," she said softly, giving me a quick hug. Then off she ran.

Neither Lena nor Mom said anything on the way home. Mom just smiled in a very irritating way, while Lena looked out the window. The parcel on my lap felt like it was smoldering.

Back at home, I ran straight up to my room. There was no way I was going to open Birgit's present in front of everyone else down in the living room at Christmas.

It was a picture. I recognized all the mountaintops. She'd painted the view from the cairn in shades of a summer's evening. You could see Kobbholmen out at sea in the evening sun, and just next to it she'd painted a black dot. That was probably *Troll*.

If anybody had seen me there in my room, they would've thought I'd gone completely bonkers. I jumped around like a fool, bumping into the shelves so hard that the ice-cream tub holding the broken bottle Lena had given me leaped off and landed on the floor. Birgit had given me a Christmas present!

Part Three

Winter and Waiting

CHAPTER TWENTY-TWO

"Away in a Manger"

*B*irgit went to the Netherlands to spend Christmas with her brothers, and suddenly I had all the time in the world. The same went for my little brother in Mom's tummy. It seemed he wasn't planning on coming out anytime soon, even if Mom was so pregnant that the walls were buckling around us. She even said that Lena was right: she was too old to have a baby.

The weather outside was really miserable, so the whole family was pretty much stuck indoors, but we did all we could to pull ourselves together to make things as comfortable as possible for Mom. For instance, I would come into the kitchen and suddenly find Magnus making dinner, or Minda playing animal bingo with Krølla instead of staring at her phone and being grumpy. As for Dad, he put up decorations, ironed tablecloths, sorted out clothes and goodness knows what else. If we absolutely had to argue, we did it in the attic, and as quietly as possible.

"Could Mom burst?" Krølla whispered while we were loading the dishwasher one evening.

She was holding a fork in her hand and looking worriedly at Mom's enormous bump.

"*Pfft*," I said dismissively.

But, secretly, I was watching Mom anxiously too. Didn't that baby realize he had to come out soon before she keeled over?

I saw unusually little of Lena. Ylva was probably keeping her at home so there would be as much peace and quiet as possible in our house. But when Boxing Day arrived and there was still no sign of our new brother, she came stomping into our kitchen in her familiar style. Outside, the wind was blowing the cold December rain sideways.

"Today we're going to go caroling, and we're going to dress up as guerrilla soldiers," she declared, wiping the worst of the rain from her face.

There was already a large puddle on the kitchen floor around where she was standing.

"Are we?" I asked skeptically.

"It's a genius idea, Trille. We'll wear Magnus's military gear and camouflage our faces. And we can borrow his hunting knife too!"

I could see several problems with what she'd said, including the fact that my big brother's name had come up twice. But I needn't have worried.

"Over my dead body!" said Mom, leaning heavily on the kitchen counter. "There's no way you and Lena are going around wearing military gear and singing 'Away in a Manger' while brandishing a hunting knife."

She told us that Christmas was a time of peace and that we should dress up as angels or Christmas elves and behave ourselves.

We went up to my room. The wind and the rain were even louder up there. Lena scanned the walls. I could see that she'd spotted the picture from Birgit.

"Kai-Tommy got one too," she muttered.

"Got what?"

"A Christmas present from Birgit."

"Oh." My voice was indifferent, but inside it felt as if the blood had stopped in my veins.

Was it true? I'd had such a happy and warm feeling all Christmas every time I'd looked at the picture! Had Birgit given Christmas presents to everybody? Or just to Kai-Tommy and me? Why did Lena have to come here and tell me this, anyway?

Angrily, I rested my chin on my palms and peered through the rain-spattered windowpane. The wind was doing its best to shake the lights off the cedar tree out in the yard. Two crooked figures were coming up the track. Grandpa and Dad. They'd been down to see to the boats.

"I can't be bothered to go caroling in this awful weather," I mumbled.

I'd grown so used to Lena just shrugging and leaving me to do my own thing recently that I was really taken aback by her reaction.

She stood right in front of me. "There's no such thing as bad weather, you wimp, only bad clothes.

160

How many of your Christmas sweets have you got left, anyway?"

"Wimp?" I asked in disbelief. Lena had hit where it hurt most. "Only snotty little brats go caroling, Lena. I'm not coming!"

Lena's eyes narrowed and she focused on something behind me instead of looking straight at me. If I wanted to stay inside playing the piano and staring at art, that was fine by her, she said coldly. It was my life. But she was going out caroling before every Tom, Didrik, and Harald went out and the sweet supplies ran dry. Then she left.

I stood there, feeling regret and anger at the same time. Eventually I pulled the sheet off my bed and stormed after her.

"OK," I said, wrapping the sheet around my shoulders.

Lena looked at me crossly. It was almost dark now.

"Are you seriously going as an angel?"

"I'm going to disguise myself as an angel," I said. "When we get up to the main road, I'm going to turn into a ghost."

I fetched a sheet for her too.

Down in the kitchen, two new puddles had appeared next to the one Lena had made when she arrived. Dad and Grandpa were shivering after their walk down to the sea.

"'God rest you merry, gentlemen,'" Lena said in greeting, curtsying in her angel costume.

"You can forget that," said Dad. "Nobody's going out this evening."

The wind was supposed to be getting stronger, he told us. On the radio, they'd been telling people to avoid going outside unless it was really urgent.

"I know one thing that's really urgent," said Lena when Grandpa and Dad had gone to get changed. "And that's my supply of goodies."

Silently, I went to fetch the waterproof cooler bag from the pantry, and then we crept out.

CHAPTER TWENTY-THREE

Hurricane Angels

We realized right away that we'd have to forget our ghost plan. If we wanted to keep the sheets over our heads, we'd have needed to tie them to the ground. The only solution was to wrap them around ourselves tightly and do our best to look like angels.

"Gales and pouring rain," Lena shouted. "It feels so Christmassy."

I was still mulling over what she'd said about Kai-Tommy. I shielded my angry face from the rain and stomped through the wind.

*   *   *

Our first caroling stop was Uncle Tor's place.

"Are you two completely crackers? Get home, for crying out loud!" he said when he opened the door, only to be met by a faceful of wind, rain, and "Away in a Manger."

"We'll go home soon," said Lena, opening the cooler bag. "We've just got to get enough to cover the bottom."

My uncle grunted as he threw in some assorted sweets and fled back indoors.

We probably should have gone home, but I didn't want to. What would I do there anyway? Sit looking at the picture Birgit had given me and tiptoe around Mom? We took shelter around the back of the hay barn so we could discuss our next move. Down by the ferry landing there was a whole bunch of houses sure to be full of sweets. It was only a quarter of an hour's walk, and there could hardly be any competition from other carolers wandering around on an evening like that.

"Imagine if we knocked on Kai-Tommy's door," said Lena. "I'd like to see his face when he realizes that we've snapped up the whole area while he's been inside waiting for snow and robins flying around."

I tightened my grip on the cooler bag handle. "Let's go," I said firmly.

Blinking barnacles, it was so good to get out and about! We practically flew along with the wind behind us. The lampposts waved in the wind, and the shadows of the tall spruce trees on the uphill side of the road danced wildly in the changing light. When we got to Ellisiv's house, I was all ready to sing a carol, but Lena thought we should press on and get these houses done first.

"We can do her on the way back!" she shouted.

We came around the headland before the ferry landing and could hear the sea roaring. The water droplets landing on our faces were salty. The storm was really picking up now. Sometimes it felt as if the wind had taken hold of me by the waist and was carrying me along the road.

"Let's do 'Joy to the World.' It's one of the shortest!" Lena shouted. She started running up toward the houses. Her sheet flapped over her shoulders like a load of confused laundry.

* * *

Generally speaking, people were quite alarmed
when they opened their doors. Lena thought their
bewilderment meant they were giving us more
sweets. We were raking in the goodies!

"I knew it had to be some of you hardy folk from
Mathildewick Cove," said Thunderclap Kåre. Clearly
impressed, he gave us each an enormous bar of
milk chocolate. "Say hello to Lars from me, and get
yourselves home!"

But we couldn't go home until we'd knocked on
Kai-Tommy's door.

The house where Kai-Tommy and his family live
looks kind of American. They even have columns by
the front door. In their yard, a thousand Christmas
lights danced in the wind.

It was his brother who opened the door, the one
who's a budding soccer talent. He was wearing a
light-blue shirt that fitted him tightly across the
chest, and he flicked his bangs back in just the
same way Kai-Tommy does. I could imagine him
wearing a soccer uniform. Minda would probably

have swooned. Was this what Kai-Tommy was going to look like in a couple of years? Was that why Birgit liked him? Dispirited, I stared down at my boots, which were sticking out from under my sheet, but Lena looked straight at Kai-Tommy's brother and started singing "Joy to the World," the song echoing through the roomy hallway.

Halfway through the verse, Kai-Tommy popped up behind his brother. For a split second, he looked at us in shock and awe, but then he put on his usual sneering face, as if we were the two greatest idiots in the world. Then the boys' parents appeared. Their mother was wearing a red Christmas dress, and Ivar looked like an English football manager, wearing a suit.

Lena's last "heaven and nature sing" was a little quieter under the gaze of her soccer coach. But when Kai-Tommy's mom brought us two large chocolate Santas, Lena opened the lid of the cooler bag ever so slightly and said, "We'll have to take them in our pockets, Trille. It's full up in here."

As we closed the door, I was pleased to hear Kai-Tommy inside, shouting, "How come they're allowed out and I'm not?"

"You'd think they had no parents," his mother replied.

"I think we should go home now, Lena," I said.

The wind and rain had crept all the way through to our skin, and now the cold had more of a bite to it. I wasn't angry anymore, just fed up and worn out. It was quite different walking against the wind. It felt like walking straight into a living wall, and sometimes it was almost hard to breathe. The best thing we could do was to lean forward and walk kind of sideways, each with an arm in front of our faces.

The way home suddenly seemed endless. A little worry started gnawing away at my stomach. What had we gotten ourselves into this time?

But it was only when we arrived back at the ferry landing that we really understood the seriousness of the situation. Lena was blown off her feet like a paper angel. Then the ice-cold sea spray came washing right up onto the road, making me lose my footing too. By the time we got up, we were both without our sheets. As if on command, we scrambled down into the ditch on the uphill side of the road.

"We have to get to the other side of the headland," I yelled.

We half walked, half crept along the wet ditch, Lena dragging the cooler bag behind her like an anchor. I remembered that her hand was still in a cast, and I turned around to take the bag. At that moment, a huge wave came roaring over the road where we'd just been, washing away stones, snow poles, and anything else that wasn't tied down. A storm surge! The fear struck me like a hammer blow. I didn't know the wind could get so much stronger so quickly!

Another gust forced us to get down almost flat in the ditch. I hardly dared look at the lampposts anymore. What if they snapped?

"Trille! Over there!"

I lifted my head. One of the spruce trees farther up the road was about to come down. The wind pulled and tore at the tree's winter-green branches, and it started to give way in slow motion. It rocked and swayed and eventually fell right over in the stormy light, like a wounded giant. We sat in the ditch, speechless, as we stared at the enormous tree lying right across the road. We were out in tree-toppling storm winds!

Then it got dark. I don't mean dark like it normally gets at night. I mean pitch-dark like in a dark closet in a dark room with a dark hallway outside. The streetlights went out, the dots of light on the other side of the fjord disappeared, and the moon fled as far away as it could. I fumbled my way over to Lena.

If we kept crawling onward, we might get mashed underneath a tree. If we crawled back to the houses where we'd been, we might get washed out to sea.

We were trapped!

CHAPTER TWENTY-FOUR

Ellisiv, Axel, and the Big Question

*E*llisiv's house!" Lena shouted in my ear.

We knew our teacher's red-painted house was all there was between the headland and the trees, but we couldn't see a thing, and it felt dangerous to crawl out of the ditch. Another blast of wind came thundering in from the sea. Then it let up slightly, so I wiped the rain from my eyes and spun my head to try to find some kind of landmark. Was this what it was like being blind?

Then something pierced the darkness like a nail.

"There!" shouted Lena.

It had to be one of Ellisiv's windows. Had she lit a candle or something? We started to fumble our way forward again. We lay down flat in the ditch every time a gust of wind came, but we dragged ourselves onward in the small gaps between the gusts. Lena went in front, while I followed behind with the bag. Eventually the house was right above us. Now we just had to climb up out of the ditch and into the yard.

We waited until the wind calmed, and then we booked it. We tripped several times. It was impossible to see where we were putting our feet, and the wind shook and ripped at us with enormous power. When we reached the house, I tripped on the bottom step and fell down flat. It hurt so much that I howled with pain, and I could taste warm blood as it trickled down from my nose and into my mouth. Another gust almost blew us back down into the yard, but finally I managed to claw my way to the door handle. I had to use all my strength to stop the door from blowing off its hinges. Then we plunged into the hallway, the door slamming behind us with a loud bang.

The sight that met Ellisiv would probably have scared most people stiff. Two soaking-wet and bloodstained children lying amid piles of chocolate and clementines. She let out a scream and put her hand to her mouth in shock. Luckily she wasn't alone. Axel, our old soccer coach, popped up from behind her. Lena and I dragged ourselves up until we were sitting.

"What are you doing here?" said Lena, looking at Axel in surprise.

"You're one to talk!" Ellisiv shouted. "What on earth are you doing, Trille and Lena?"

"Well, we were going to sing you a Christmas carol, but . . ." Lena couldn't go on.

Then I felt it too. I was overcome with cold and fear, and my whole body was shivering.

I'm not sure I'll ever be able to explain what it was like to take that steaming-hot cup of warm squash in my hands. The wind was roaring against the walls outside, but Lena and I were sitting close together on an old sofa, propped up with cushions and wrapped in blankets. Our wet clothes were hanging over by the stove, making the windows steam up. The lovely squash sent waves of warmth through my body.

"Thanks," I mumbled, which was the first word I had been able to say. "We need to phone home," I added.

"The signal's down," said Axel.

Oh no! Dad was going to be worried to death! And Mom! This was the last thing she needed.

"I just managed to send a message before the network blacked out," said Ellisiv when she saw how panicked I was. "They know you're safe."

I've been through stormy nights before. Not every year, but often enough to know what it's like at home. Dad paces anxiously, wondering if the barn, the boats, and everything else are all right, while Mom keeps on saying that there's nothing they can do but wait. As a rule, when the wind's really strong—when the storms are big enough to have names—then we're ordered to go down to Grandpa's apartment in the basement. That's where it's safest. It's not like my bedroom in the attic, where you can hear the roof tiles rattling above your head. Were my family down in Grandpa's apartment now? Were they able to relax now they knew Lena and I were here? Were they really, really angry?

Axel put more wood on the fire. He clearly knew what he was doing with that massive stove. More gusts of wind shook and tore at the house. Lena had been blue with cold when we arrived there, but the warm squash put life back in her. Now her cheeks were as red as Santa's. She looked at Ellisiv, then at Axel, and then back at Ellisiv again.

"So, Axel. Haven't you got a girlfriend in town?" she asked eventually.

I'd forgotten to tell her! Ellisiv went bright red, and Axel cleared his throat.

"She dumped him," I whispered to Lena, hoping that she might start talking about the weather instead. That would give her plenty to talk about today of all days. But no.

"So are you two boyfriend and girlfriend now?"

I looked down at my squash in embarrassment.

"Well, I don't know about that," Ellisiv mumbled.

Axel stopped poking the fire. "What?" he said. "Aren't we boyfriend and girlfriend? What are we, then?"

"Well . . ." said Ellisiv, her face turning redder than that time when we were nine and Lena had punched Kai-Tommy in the middle of the classroom.

A very awkward silence spread through the room. Luckily the wind was really raging outside.

Lena took a swig of her squash.

"You two would make a good couple, anyway," she said eventually, just to settle the matter. "Can we offer you a few pounds of chocolate?"

We swept up our haul from the hallway floor and laid it out on the table. While we were doing that, Axel spotted Lena's soggy plaster cast.

"I think it might be best if we took that cast off," he said.

"Yes." Lena nodded. "It was supposed to be coming off on the third of January, anyway."

Ellisiv fetched some scissors and a knife. Soon Lena was stretching out her fingers in a way she hadn't been able to for some time.

"Now you're ready to stand in goal again," said Axel, giving her a pat on the back.

That was enough to make Lena fall silent. She closed her lips tightly, as if she hadn't heard what he'd said.

"It's mainly Halvor who stands in goal now," I said.

Axel looked at Lena, confused. "Aren't you the goalie anymore?"

Lena took one of the chocolate bars that Thunderclap Kåre had given us and broke it up into pieces with short, sharp snaps.

"Lena?" Axel wasn't giving up.

"You bet your cod liver oil I'm a goalie. I just don't have a goal to stand in," she said.

Lena had been grumbling and moaning about soccer practice to everybody back in Mathildewick Cove, and we'd all listened with half an ear, waiting for it to blow over. Now I saw two grown adults get almost as worked up about the situation as Lena herself. Axel leaned over the table and asked her all about the practices with Ivar and the boys, and Lena reluctantly told him how life had been on the field over the last few months.

"But that's not fair, Lena," said Ellisiv. "Even I know you're a good goalie."

Axel nodded. "It's not right, Lena."

He seemed genuinely angry about how Lena had been treated. I felt a pang of guilt. Why hadn't I been angry?

"What would you think about starting to play in town?" Axel asked.

"Huh?" said Lena.

"I know Lash, the man who trains the girls two years older than you. They've been struggling to find a decent goalie this season. Would you like to try out with them?"

"On a girls' team?" said Lena, as if he'd suggested that she should play with a team of camels.

"Well, you are a girl, Lena," Ellisiv said dryly. "If you're going to carry on playing soccer, sooner or later you'll have to join a girls' team."

I was sure Lena would say no. No way would she dare to change teams! Deep in thought, she wolfed down five pieces of chocolate.

"Which days do they practice on?" she asked eventually.

I glanced at her sideways, surprised. Was she really that brave? I wasn't sure if it was a pang of envy I was feeling, or something else.

* * *

As the night wore on, the weather worsened. There was no longer any doubt that this was a hurricane. Axel paced around the small living room nervously, and at one point he went out onto the doorstep, but he quickly came back indoors.

"This house has stood here since the eighteen hundreds," said Ellisiv, "so I'm sure it'll last tonight too."

She drew Lena close in the crook of her arm, in the way only Ellisiv can, and they fell asleep there on the sofa.

CHAPTER TWENTY-FIVE

After the Storm

The wind dropped early the next morning. At daybreak, we went outside and stood on the doorstep, speechless. It was as if the world had been through the fight of its life and was now gasping for breath. Ellisiv's plum tree had snapped right in two, leaving sharp white splinters. Farther toward Mathildewick Cove, fallen spruce trees littered the road, and in some spots, pieces of the asphalt surface had been washed away. One of the lampposts down below the house was clumsily curtsying to us. Behind all of this was the ocean, a gray, seasick mass.

The thought of Lena and me having been out in all this made me feel very queasy. Down at the shore, big, restless breakers rolled onto the land, throwing up branches and debris between the rocks.

"I wonder what it was like on Kobbholmen last night," Lena said, full of thought. "Do you think the house is still standing?"

Before I could answer, we heard the sound of a tractor. It stopped a bit up the road, unable to get any farther. Somebody leaped out and started scrambling over the fallen spruce trees. It was Dad.

"Trille!"

When he finally reached the house I was captured in a bear hug. After a moment, he swept Lena into the same hug. Wasn't he angry?

"Is it safe to be out in the tractor before they've cleared the road?" Lena asked.

Dad let go of her. "Safe?" he shouted. "You've got some nerve asking that, after you went strolling around caroling in the middle of Armageddon!"

He was angry. Extremely angry.

"Where's Isak?" Lena asked meekly.

I could hear in her voice that she would have

liked him to be the one to come along in the tractor and give us a bear hug.

"Isak?" Dad clasped his hands together. "Isak's with Kari, Lena! Trille became a big brother again overnight!"

My brother had chosen the stormiest night in living memory to be born. A night when huge trees had blocked the road so no ambulance could get through. A night when the ferry couldn't sail. And a night when the phones and emergency networks were down, so nobody could call anyone.

While the hurricane winds blasted our cove again and again, Mom had given birth to a whole new person down in Grandpa's apartment. The storm had made Isak the midwife and Ylva the nurse. Minda and Magnus had run around the apartment like mad, fetching towels and water, stoking the fires and keeping an eye on the candles. And Grandpa, who rarely got worked up about anything, had been wandering around like a nervous wreck, ranting and raving, puzzling over who on earth had the great idea that women should go through so much pain when they were having children. Krølla was the only one who'd slept through the whole drama.

"And it wasn't a brother after all, Trille," said Dad, his voice all puffed up, when we'd clambered carefully over the fallen trees and gotten into the tractor.

He turned the key very energetically. "It's a sister, folks! A big, strong, round bundle of a sister!"

Grandpa had weighed her at once on his fishing scale: 4,790 grams—more than ten and a half pounds!

"Do you realize what a mother you've got?" Dad shouted wildly, pinching my cheek so hard it hurt. "Do you realize?"

Did I realize what a mother I'd got? I stood there, peeping around the corner of the bedroom door. She was as peaceful as Dad was half-mad. Her gray bangs curled delicately over her forehead. She looked like she was resting after some kind of hurricane too. Krølla was sitting next to the bed, sparkling like the sun. You could see from her glow that she was now a big sister.

"Trille dear," Mom said softly when I went in, stroking my cheek. "What on earth were you thinking?"

I was about to answer, but she clearly wasn't that upset.

"Look," she just said, nodding toward the cradle. "Feel free to pick her up."

"She hardly weighs anything," Krølla said from the other side of the cradle.

"Well, I don't know about that," Mom mumbled, clearly worn out, laying her head back on the pillow.

I carefully picked up this little person. I was a fair bit younger when Krølla was born, and I don't remember all that much about it, so I was quite unprepared for what it would feel like to hold my new little sister in my arms. She more or less just crawled into my heart and made herself comfortable. If she'd ordered me to do a book presentation, I would've done it. That's how it felt. Outside, the wind had turned everything upside down, but here she lay, peaceful and safe, and new to the world. It was incredible!

I'll always look after you, I thought, looking at

her round, red face and half-open mouth.

Lena came in silently behind me. She looked at the little girl with a serious expression and shook her head slightly when I asked if she wanted to hold her. Instead she gently stroked one of her strong, stringy fingers over the top of the baby's nose. Then she sighed and left.

It was strange having no electricity or Internet connection, but quite good too. Later in the day, Ylva and Dad warmed up some Christmas leftovers on the living-room stove and managed to throw together a meal for everybody. Magnus was the only one who interrogated Lena and me about our caroling expedition. I was pleased it was lost in all the fuss, although we'd probably hear more about it when things calmed down.

"Has she got a name?" I asked when we were all gathered around the table, and Mom was feeding my little sister in the armchair by the stove.

I'd been a little worried about this aspect. Neither Krølla nor I think we've been especially lucky with our names. There's a reason we're known by our nicknames, put it that way. Mom and Dad exchanged looks.

"We're thinking about calling her something to do with wind and hurricanes," said Mom.

"Such as?" Magnus asked skeptically.

"Stormetta," said Dad. "Do you like it?"

Minda stopped chewing and looked at Magnus. He coughed slightly. Stormetta. It was certainly unusual, but we could probably get used to it. In a way, it's a good thing to have a name that not so many people have. We nodded and shrugged. Stormetta. It would do.

"If I were you, I'd call her something else," said Lena from the other end of the table.

"Lena!" said Ylva angrily.

Sometimes I think Lena forgets that she's not one of my siblings too.

Mom chuckled quietly over in her chair. "What do you think she should be called, then?"

Lena swallowed what she was eating and looked at Grandpa.

"I think Inger would be better."

CHAPTER TWENTY-SIX

Flotsam and Jetsam

*H*urricanes like the one we'd just had don't only wash up plastic drums and those scoops you use for bailing out boats. After a quick search down by the water, we'd found an escaped part of a pier, Thunderclap Kåre's plastic-hulled boat, half a playhouse, and a dead deer. The storm surge had also made a mess of the rocks from the breakwater and smashed the door of our boat shed to smithereens. Luckily, *Troll* only had some minor hull damage. All in all, it wasn't that bad in Mathildewick Cove. It was worse elsewhere.

When the electricity came back on and we were connected to the rest of the world again, messages started to stream in about all the destruction. Forests had been flattened like freshly mown grass on several mountainsides, boats and boat sheds had been battered all along the coast, and some people's houses had even been destroyed.

"When you think about it, the most incredible thing isn't that our sister arrived last night," said Magnus when we were down having a look at the breakwater. "The most epic event of the whole hurricane has to be you and Lena going out caroling. It's so insanely typical of you two."

"*Pssshh*," I said.

As usual after a storm, we trawled the beaches for storm treasure. We could've built an entire armada with all the driftwood. Lena was well on the way to designing a new, improved raft.

"The one we made last time was a piece of junk. This time we can pick the proper materials," she said, examining the rubbish on the shoreline with a critical eye.

I nodded. I could feel in my chest my enthusiasm starting to grow a tiny bit. We might actually make something incredibly good out of all this. Lena hopped happily from stone to stone.

"Huh? Trille, look!" she suddenly shouted, picking up something shiny from an enormous tangle of seaweed.

But I was no longer looking or listening, as a sight had appeared back up by our houses that made my heart skip a beat. Birgit and Haas. They came strolling down the track under the rowan trees. The sun shot orange wintry rays across the fields, making everything glitter around them. She was back!

"Happy New Year."

Birgit looked warmly at me and at the chaos on the beach. I just smiled. How good it was to see her, and how much I had to tell her! Haas bounded headlong into my stomach, and then he ran down to Lena, who was still standing by the clump of seaweed and didn't look like she was planning to move from there anytime soon.

"Lena thinks we should build another raft," I said, shrugging in exasperation.

Birgit laughed and said that she'd prefer not to.

"Me neither, really," I said, glancing down at Lena, who had just heaved half a boat-shed door up onto the grass, dropping it with a soggy smack.

Haas barked as he leaped around her.

"He's pleased to be back," said Birgit. "Mathildewick Cove is better than Amsterdam for a dog."

I wanted to ask her whether she was also pleased to be back, but I couldn't. Instead, we set off together and ambled on down to Lena.

"What was it you found?" I asked, remembering that she'd shouted something to me.

"Oh, nothing special," she grumbled without looking at me.

Then she carried on searching. I could see that she'd hidden something under her jacket, but I thought no more of it.

CHAPTER TWENTY-SEVEN

Lena Resorts to Violence

"Wh-why weren't you at practice yesterday?"

We were back at school again. It was almost time for PE and we were sitting outside the changing rooms, freezing cold. Andreas was looking at Lena with questioning eyes.

"I'm transferring," she said curtly.

All the boys stopped talking.

"Transferring? Where are you going to play, then?" Halvor asked in surprise.

"With some girls in town."

"Oh," said Andreas. "That's a sh-shame."

"Sh-sh-shame," said Kai-Tommy, imitating him. He and Halvor snickered.

Lena put her feet up on her gym bag and gave them a scowl of contempt.

"I'm not going to waste my life sitting on the bench," she muttered.

Kai-Tommy smiled. "Good idea to join the girls' team, in that case," he said. "It's more at your level."

That was it. Finally the old Lena awoke.

"There's no problem with the level, you circus llama!"

"What did you say?" Kai-Tommy leaned forward.

"I said: there's no problem with the level, you circus llama!"

Birgit looked at them in astonishment. Was she finally going to see how things worked in our class?

"What is the problem, then?" Kai-Tommy asked.

Lena didn't answer. Kai-Tommy repeated the question. He was determined to have an answer.

"The coach," said Lena eventually, looking straight at him.

Kai-Tommy started laughing. "The coach? You really don't get it, Lena!"

"What is there to get, you amoeba? I'm just as good as Halvor, and yet that father of yours has kept me on the bench the whole season. It's not fair."

"You're not as good as you think," Kai-Tommy said in mock despair. "You haven't got a chance of keeping up anymore."

"That's a load of rubbish!" Lena shouted, rising to her feet.

"A load of rubbish?"

Kai-Tommy was on his feet too. I remembered the time Lena punched him. They had been more or less the same size then. Now Kai-Tommy was much bigger.

"We're building up the team," he said. "Halvor's in goal because he's got a future as a goalie. We can't bring you on just to be nice to girls."

And so it happened again. Lena lashed out.

A gasp spread through the whole group. Kai-Tommy staggered backward, but it wasn't a knockout this time like three years earlier. He blinked a little, touched his jaw, and then launched himself furiously at Lena. For a second, the rest of us stood there, paralyzed, while they beat each other up. Big Kai-Tommy and little Lena.

"No!" I shouted, diving into the fight.

Halvor and Abdulahi grabbed Kai-Tommy.

Andreas and I got hold of Lena. We managed to separate them before the teacher came.

"You're a complete moron, Kai-Tommy!" Lena shouted. Tears were running down her cheeks, and she was bleeding from a cut above her eye. "You're a bunch of little morons, the whole herd of you."

Then she ran off.

Birgit stood outside the girls' changing rooms, pale and speechless. Kai-Tommy glanced over at her and wiped some grit from his cheek.

"That girl's a total nutcase," he mumbled, holding up his hands half-apologetically.

But what was wrong with me? I just stood there feeling pleased that finally Birgit had seen what Kai-Tommy could be like. By the time I turned to run after Lena, I realized that Andreas had already followed her.

Lena's desk was deserted for the rest of the day. There was a strangely charged atmosphere in class. Ellisiv, who didn't know what had happened, watched us with a furrowed brow. I knew that whatever she did, Lena would never, ever tell anybody what had happened. Should I tell? I decided to leave it.

When I got home, Lena had gone to soccer practice with her new team. Some days she'd have to leave straight after school to catch the ferry.

I sat down in our empty kitchen and picked at some crumbs on the table.

"Isn't Lena here?" asked Mom, who was feeding Inger in the living room.

I shook my head.

As dusk came, I stood behind the cedar tree and watched her cycling home. Should I go over to the Lids' kitchen? Was she mad at me? Blasted soccer! I wished it had never been invented.

Before I could decide what to do, her door opened again. Lena ran across the fields and down to the boat shed. I peered through the dark. There were lights on down there. Grandpa was doing some work on *Troll*. What did they talk about when they were together, Lena and Grandpa?

I turned around and went back inside.

CHAPTER TWENTY-EIGHT

My Grandfather Hands

*A*s the end of winter approached, Grandpa was always showing up wearing dirty overalls. He was working on *Troll* and was keen to get his boat ready for the next fishing season.

"Can't you wait until spring comes?" Dad asked him. "What are you going out in the cold for now?"

Grandpa pretended not to hear him. He just looked across at me and said, "I think we'll be ready in time for the cod, Trille."

I nodded and felt a guilty conscience simmering in my stomach. It was ages since I'd last been with him to the boat shed.

When he went out, Grandpa didn't stay out for very long at a time, though. My new little sister often had gas, and she couldn't whimper more than a smidgen without Grandpa dropping whatever he had in his hands and rushing to her aid.

"We need expertise here," he'd say, turning Inger so that he was holding her round belly in the palm of his hand.

Then they'd walk around the house, Grandpa and Inger, while he gently rocked her and stroked his other big hand over her little back.

"Listen to that!" he'd shout proudly at each fart and burp that came out.

He usually called her his "wee dumpling," but every now and then he'd say her name. When he did so, he said it quickly and in a slightly embarrassed voice, more or less like when Lena called Isak "Dad."

One day, I realized to my astonishment that I'd started carrying Inger like Grandpa did. My hands were smaller, but just like before in the boat shed, they were starting to act like his, even though I wasn't really doing it on purpose.

"Listen to that!" I said to Mom one day, grinning as Inger let rip with an explosive fart while I was carrying her, Grandpa-style.

"Mini-Lars," Mom said, ruffling my hair.

It was a long time since anybody had called me that.

Suddenly I had a burning need to get down to the boat shed. I leaped into my boots and ran across the fields. *Troll* was laid up ashore, and Grandpa was painting the bottom of the hull.

"Would you like any help?"

"No, you'll only get dirty," said Grandpa, looking at my clothes.

"*Pssshh*," I said. "I can put on some oilskins."

I took the orange oilskins from the hook in the boat shed. It had been ages since I'd last worn them. A faint and familiar smell of fish and seawater stuck to my body.

"Is it time to put her back in the water tomorrow?" I asked, crawling all the way underneath the boat to the hardest-to-reach part.

"Looks like it, lad," said Grandpa, looking happily at me. "Tor's promised to lend a hand."

It was so good to be lying under the boat there with Grandpa, just working away. I wished we could carry on all afternoon, but he had almost finished. The job was done in half an hour. I hung the oilskins back up, and we strolled off along the track home.

"Thanks for your help," Grandpa said with a nod.

"No problem," I said. I was just about to follow him inside when I spotted Birgit.

She was coming down from Hillside on her bike at top speed. I felt a pang of excitement in my stomach. Was she coming to see me? I was about to hurry and meet her, but then I was stunned to see her turn the other way.

I felt completely dismayed. I knew where she was going. It was getting clearer from conversations I overheard between Birgit and Kai-Tommy that they'd been hanging out at the ferry landing after school. I gulped.

"See you later, then," I mumbled to Grandpa, heading up to the garage to find my bike.

Soon I was sitting there at the ferry landing, outside the shop, dangling my legs. Mopeds roared around me while Kai-Tommy, Halvor, and a couple of high school students sat over on another table. There was no sign of Birgit. Was this not where she'd been heading after all? I'd been into the shop to look for her. Now I was sitting with a Coke in my hand, feeling like a fool.

Then Lena came along on her bike, with her soccer bag on the carrier rack and wearing a tracksuit in the unfamiliar red color of the team in town. She spotted me as she parked her bike and tilted her head as if examining a rare orchid.

"You're sitting here?"

I nodded. As if to prove the point that I was now one of the kids who sat around on the ferry landing, I leaned to one side and casually spat on the pier. Lena bit her lip. I knew her. She was trying not to laugh.

"What?" I said, holding out my arms in protest.

Lena hopped up onto the table and sat down next to me.

"You look like a moron, Trille. You've gone completely coo coo ca choo."

Oh, couldn't she just keep her trap shut?

"Hey hey! It's the two turtledoves of Mathilde-wick Cove!" Kai-Tommy shouted at us from the other side of the parking lot.

At that very moment, Birgit arrived on her bike. I was ready to shove Lena off the table. What if Birgit got the wrong idea? But Lena just sat there firmly, looking tiredly at Kai-Tommy.

"I really hope he gets washed away in a flood one day," she grumbled.

I waved to Birgit as she went into the shop.

Kai-Tommy kept gawping in our direction, and I could feel the tension growing. Ever since the fight, he'd been rotten to Lena. He'd arrogantly declared that she had serious problems with her temper—although he did have a point there—as well as saying that it wasn't normal to beat people up like she did. And to prove that he was right, he'd taken every opportunity to get her fired up again. He'd come pretty close to succeeding a few times, but amazingly Lena had managed not to explode.

Now she unzipped her tracksuit top and looked at me, eyes sparkling. She looked like she might burst at any moment.

"What is it?" I asked.

Lena smiled wide.

"What is it? Have you won a million or something?"

"We're going to have a baby," she said, her voice bursting with pent-up joy.

"Really? Is that true?"

Lena nodded with the happiest of grins on her face.

"Congratulations!"

"Congratulations for what?" Kai-Tommy had ridden his bike over to us and was now propping himself up against the table with one foot.

"Nothing," said Lena.

Kai-Tommy calmly opened his bottle of soda pop and took a swig from it. He was only wearing a hoodie, even though it was freezing cold.

"Dressed like a pro, I see," he said sarcastically, pointing at Lena's tracksuit.

Lena didn't respond. Instead she looked at the ferry, which was just docking.

"How's it going in town, then?" Kai-Tommy asked after a pause.

"Fine, thank you," Lena replied, still not taking

her eyes off the ferry. "I'm getting on well at my own level."

"Played any games yet?"

"No."

Kai-Tommy rocked a little on his bike. He seemed annoyed that he wasn't managing to wind her up.

"What was he congratulating you about, then?"

"I was congratulating her because she's going to be a big sister," I said in exasperation.

"Oh," he said, surprised. "Congrats, then."

Without thanking him, Lena stood up, ready to board the ferry. I don't know whether that was what Kai-Tommy couldn't stand, or whether it was the fact he hadn't managed to make her explode. Something snapped, anyway.

He flicked back his bangs and shouted after Lena, "Lucky Isak, getting his own kid. It can't have been easy for him with you thrown into the bargain, knowing what you're like."

I felt myself turning all cold inside. Lena didn't answer. She just went on board the ferry. Hadn't she heard? I looked furiously at Kai-Tommy, but I didn't say anything, as Birgit was coming now.

She'd bought some chocolate, which she opened and shared with us, all smiles.

"Is something wrong?" she asked hesitantly.

I looked nervously at the ferry. Didn't Lena care about what Kai-Tommy had just said? She was Isak's child too! She knew that, didn't she? Kai-Tommy peered at me from beneath his bangs, and then he suddenly started sniffing the air.

"Something smells of flipping fish here."

All the blood drained to my feet. I quickly glanced at Birgit. She cautiously sniffed the air too.

"Seriously, Trille, is that you?" Kai-Tommy looked at me as if I were the most repulsive person in the world.

"No," I said, pulling back.

I quickly downed the rest of my drink and leaped onto my bike. My whole body felt like it was burning and throbbing with shame.

When I got home, I threw my bike in the garage and almost walked straight into Grandpa. He was outside the house, with a bucket of frozen herring, on his way to the boat shed.

"Are you coming, Trille?" he asked.

"No," I grumbled, running indoors with my heart pounding.

I hurled all my clothes in with the rest of the laundry and got into the shower, devastated.

CHAPTER TWENTY-NINE

The Death of a Chicken

*T*he next day, I kept my distance from Birgit. I was too embarrassed to talk to her ever again, fish-face that I was. Kai-Tommy smirked and held his nose when I walked past him. If I hadn't been so deep in my own misery, I would probably have noticed that things weren't right with Lena either. But I didn't.

When evening came and Lena started sobbing because of a deceased hen, I still didn't see that there was really something else going on. I should have noticed, but what happened with the chicken led to such enormous complications that Lena completely fell off my radar.

* * *

It started when Birgit popped by. In astonishment,
I let her into the kitchen, ashamed that the dirty
dishes from dinner were still on the table.

"You can bring Haas in too," I mumbled, but she
left him outside.

"I won't stay long," she said, glancing at me.

No, and I can understand why, I thought.

Birgit looked at me with her kind eyes and was
just about to say something when Haas suddenly
started barking.

"Oh no, it must be the fox!"

I charged out of the kitchen. We'd already lost two
hens over the past month. Dad kept saying that he
was going to keep watch one morning and shoot the
sneaky creature when it ventured down to the farm,
but so far he'd only talked about it. When the first
hen, Number Two B, disappeared, we didn't get too
worked up about it. Nor did we when Number Five
vanished, leaving just a few feathers and some drops
of blood. But that evening was different. I knew that
much as soon as I came rushing out into the yard.
Lena was already there, and she was absolutely raging.

Number Seven, her favorite hen, was lying on her back right up by the chicken-wire fence. Her head was wounded, but she was still alive. The fox had probably been scared off in the middle of the massacre when Haas started barking. Lena bent down, and when she stood up with the hen in her arms, she was sobbing so hard I was shocked. What on earth? It was only a chicken!

"Lena," I said gently, "she's too badly injured to survive. You can't . . ."

"I know. I'm not an idiot!"

She turned around, walked straight over to the door to Grandpa's apartment, and rang the bell. I could hear her sniffing as she tried to pull herself together. Grandpa turned on the outside light and opened the door.

"Can you help me see this one off, Lars?" Lena asked, holding the hen out in the light.

I should probably have realized then that this wasn't an everyday occurrence for Birgit. If I'd turned around, I would've seen that she was twice as pale as when we had the shipwreck on the raft.

But at that moment I was mostly thinking about Lena and the hen.

Grandpa gave Number Seven a quick and clean end, as only he can.

"Now, why don't we see if Reidar can make some chicken fricassee this weekend?" he consoled us, holding the hen up to the outside light to check she was definitely dead.

I heard a gasp behind me and finally turned toward Birgit.

"What's chicken fricassee?" she whispered, her eyes still fixed on the hen beneath the light.

I explained it like I explained all new words to her.

"It's a meal. Pieces of chicken in a white sauce. Very tasty."

Birgit's eyes shone wide in the dark. "But . . . Lena's crying," she spluttered, looking over at Lena, who was carrying the chicken's bloodstained carcass up the stairs to Mom in the kitchen.

It's good to make food out of the animals we have to put down: that's what Dad had always said, and that's what I told Birgit now. She gaped at me as if I came from another solar system.

"Is it better to eat animals you don't know?" I asked, confused.

"I don't eat animals," Birgit whispered.

"Huh?"

"We're vegetarians, you know . . ."

"Oh," I said, gobsmacked. I hadn't picked up on that. "So you never eat meat?"

Birgit shook her head.

"What about fish?"

She shook her head again.

"But what do you eat, then?" I asked in confusion, as all the dinners I'd ever eaten in my life had involved either fish or meat.

"Other things!" Birgit said angrily, and then she ran off home with Haas.

I stood there in the yard, my whole body feeling powerless. With heavy footsteps, I followed the trail of blood indoors.

The scene in the kitchen was chaos. Lena was crying her eyes out, and Mom was doing her best to comfort her while she warmed up some water in a large pot on the stove.

"Is Reidar going to shoot that fox soon, or is he just bragging?" Lena shouted. I'd never seen anybody so upset before.

"Oh, Lena dear," said Mom, trying to get hold of her.

Lena tore herself away. "It's Number Seven!"

Mom knew that. She took the hen and dipped her in the hot water for a moment.

"Do you two want to help me pluck the feathers?" she asked.

"No!" Lena howled.

I looked sadly at the hen. Chicken fricassee with potatoes and boiled carrots is one of the best meals I know of. It was one of Granny's dishes. It's something really special. Did Birgit think it was disgusting?

"Smoking haddocks, I know what I'm going to do," Lena mumbled, wiping her eyes with the sleeve of her sweater. "Come on, Trille."

I should've cycled up to Hillside and spoken with Birgit, but I couldn't face it. Instead I took my bike and followed Lena. I'd been eating animals I loved all my life. The same bottle lambs I fed in the summer, I ate at Christmas. The rabbits that lived under Grandpa's kitchen window had been turned into soup, one by one. We ate our goat, and we'd had frequent banquets from our chickens. And fish! I'd eaten enough fish to fill a whole swimming pool. Never in my life had I thought that there might be anything wrong with it. Now Birgit, dear, kind Birgit, had stormed off home in horror and disgust. I remembered the beautiful vegetable garden they had up at Hillside. And the sourdough bread with chanterelle mushrooms I'd been given. She thought I was horrible. I smelled of fish, ate animals, and was an utterly revolting person.

As this merry-go-round of thoughts spun in my head, I pedaled on hard to keep up with Lena. Soon we were at the houses by the ferry landing.

"What are we doing?" I asked with a sigh when Lena came skidding to a halt by Halvor's house.

She didn't answer. She just threw her bike into the hedge and rang the doorbell without mercy. Halvor opened the door.

"I need to borrow your air rifle," said Lena. "You'll get it back at school tomorrow."

Halvor held his lips tightly closed and looked like he was focusing on something slightly behind her. Once again I had the impression he was a little scared of her.

When we cycled home, Lena had the rifle over her shoulder.

CHAPTER THIRTY

Lena Shoots Dad in the Bum

*H*ello, I'm talking to you! Have you had a brain anesthetic or something?" Lena asked.

"Huh?"

"I said: Can you bring Reidar's mountain poncho so we've got something to camouflage ourselves with?"

"You can't kill foxes with air rifles," I replied, annoyed.

Lena wasn't planning on killing it, she told me. She just wanted to scare it. The fox couldn't be allowed to keep swaggering around and killing innocent civilian hens who'd never done anything except lay eggs and go tobogganing.

"When it hears the bang of the air rifle, it'll realize."

"Lena, I don't think that—"

"You'll see!" she roared.

It had started raining, but Lena used a tarp to make a little hunting shelter behind the corner of the hay barn. When I arrived with the poncho, she was sitting astride a folding chair, her face locked in concentration and daubed with camouflage paint. The rifle was lying on her leg, and on a small table beside her was a towering stack of chocolate-spread sandwiches and a pair of binoculars. She looked totally crazy. Normally I would've laughed, but not that day.

I plonked myself down next to her and laid the green-and-brown poncho over our legs. Neither of us said a word. We just stared somberly at the chicken run.

Suddenly, after only half an hour, we heard sounds coming from over there. Lena lifted the air rifle and fired off a shot at the moving shape.

"*Aaaaargh!* What the—?"

A large shadow stood up inside the chicken run.

"Smoking haddocks, I've shot Reidar," Lena whispered.

"Lena? Trille?!"

We sprinted off across the dark fields, sending slush splattering around us.

"Let's hide in the boat," Lena said, panting. "We can lock it from inside."

She was already heading out onto the floating pier inside the breakwater, where *Troll* was afloat for the first time since the hurricane. We clambered aboard and slammed the cabin hatch shut.

For a while, we stayed frozen in the darkness and listened. We heard Dad calling angrily a couple of times, and then there was silence. I felt tired, so I crawled along to the innermost bunk and lay down, exhausted. The smells and sounds in the cabin reminded me of the summer, of Grandpa, of the sea and peaceful times. It was like returning to an old country we'd left behind.

I heard Lena rummaging around in the cupboards,

and she soon appeared in the darkness, bringing some cookies.

"These were probably well past their sell-by date before we were even born," she muttered, stuffing one in her mouth. "Are there any blankets here?"

I thought of all the times Lena and I had sat like that, talking about all sorts of things. Now we were both completely silent. We listened to the waves lapping beneath the boat as we wrestled with our own thoughts, and the dark slowly swallowed all that was left of the day.

"I've got to go now," Lena said eventually, her teeth chattering. "I can't catch a chill with all the season's games still to play."

She got the air rifle ready and opened the cabin hatch. Was she going to shoot Dad again?

"I'll stay here a bit longer," I mumbled.

Maybe I could catch a chill? I thought hopefully, tucking myself into the blankets Lena had warmed up.

With the rain drumming down outside and the waves lapping against the side of the boat, I fell asleep.

CHAPTER THIRTY-ONE

Grandpa, the Sea, and Me

J could've been offended that neither Mom nor Dad noticed I was gone until the next morning. But there are so many of us in the Danielsen Yttergård family, it can be hard to keep track of everyone. Dad's bum hurt, and Inger had been screaming all evening. Each of my parents thought that the other had said good night to me.

But they hadn't, because I was lying asleep in Grandpa's boat, with a woolen blanket over my head. When I woke up, *Troll* was swaying in a different way from the night before, and the engine was running. I sat up in a daze. The gray morning light was seeping through the cabin hatch, and I caught a few glimpses of Grandpa's blue overalls out on deck. Was it morning? Grandpa was talking on the phone. That was what had woken me. He always holds his cell phone a short distance away from his head, as if it's a crab that he's worried might bite his ear.

"Eh?" he was shouting. "No, Trille's not on board . . ."

I was about to creep out, but Grandpa was busy.

"Half the line's in the water, Reidar. I've got to go! Call me back if you can't find him."

Then he hung up and tossed the phone into the cabin. It landed right next to me. I felt a lump in my stomach right away. I remembered Birgit's face when Grandpa had killed the hen. And Kai-Tommy mockingly turning up his nose. The very thought of going to school made me feel queasy. With my stiff fingers, I picked up Grandpa's phone and wrote a message to Dad. *I'm in the boat. Sorry that you got shot.*

Then I turned it off and plunged back under the blankets. I felt like a little jellyfish. I could imagine Dad going berserk when he read the message, but I couldn't summon the energy to care. They could go ahead and shout at me. I couldn't take any more. The throbbing of *Troll*'s engine mixed with my pounding heart. I quietly tucked myself in more tightly and drifted off to sleep again. I didn't want to think any more about anything.

Several hours had passed when I suddenly awoke. Somebody was yelling!

I've heard lots of yelling in my life. Lena frequently yells, and so do the rest of my family sometimes. Every one of them. But I'd never heard Grandpa yell before. That's why I couldn't immediately work out what I was hearing. And when I did realize, it was as if a rockslide had slammed straight into me.

I threw the blankets aside and leaped out through the cabin hatch. The gray daylight blinded me. The deck was covered in fish blood, and Grandpa was leaning over the winch. He yelled again. And then I saw it: his hand was stuck, and the blood on the deck had nothing to do with any fish.

"Grandpa!" I shouted.

I saw him jump when he heard my voice.

"Trille?"

He couldn't turn around. I reached up and switched off the winch.

"The knife . . ." Grandpa spluttered. "On the deck . . . You've got to cut . . . the line."

The knife, the knife. Where was it? My hands scrabbled around in my grandfather's blood and the rainwater. I eventually found it in the shadow of the fish tub.

"Got it!" I shouted.

Grandpa didn't answer. I was afraid he'd black out, but he nodded at the line. It was drawn taut straight down into the sea. Something was pulling at it with immense force.

When I got to the railing, I saw something I'll never forget: there was a monster next to the boat. A white body, almost as long as *Troll* herself, shone at me from the water below. The halibut was writhing around on the hook, using its enormous strength to try to free itself. The whole boat shook.

"Grandpa . . ." I whispered.

The giant fish was pulling and pulling as it tried to swim back down into the dark waters. Were there really such big creatures down there?

I turned toward Grandpa. His face was gray, and he just gave me a brief nod.

Then I cut the line with the knife. All the strain was gone. The huge, beautiful fish vanished into the depths below, and Grandpa sank down onto the deck.

CHAPTER THIRTY-TWO

A Heroic Deed

*I*t was as if life had all been a game up until that day. Whatever mess I got myself into, there was always an adult who would sort things out. But that day on *Troll*, the only adult was lying lifeless in his own blood. We were surrounded by rough seas. I could've shouted my lungs out and nobody would've heard. It was just me, Trille Danielsen Yttergård, and the sea.

I don't know how long I stood there with the knife in my hand, as if I'd been switched off. But, eventually, something inside me gave me a kick in the backside. I had to get Grandpa ashore!

I whipped off my sweater and wound my white T-shirt around Grandpa's shattered arm. Then I rushed into the cabin and found an old sheet, which I wrapped around it again. His arm now looked like a ball. I didn't risk moving Grandpa into the cabin. Instead I dragged all the blankets out and managed to put two down beneath him and two covering him. As I unfolded the last blanket, Grandpa's cell phone suddenly slipped out onto the deck, then under the railing, and into the sea with a plop.

"No!"

I ran to the side of the boat, but I could only see bubbles where the phone had disappeared.

Troll danced and drifted over the gray sea swells. The shore was endlessly distant, wrapped in clouds of mist and squalls of rain. There were no other boats to be seen. I gritted my teeth and started the engine. I couldn't head to Mathildewick Cove. We were closer to town — where the hospital was.

I'd been out with Grandpa on *Troll* a billion times, but he'd never taught me how to make emergency calls on the radio. Why had he never done that? And why didn't he have an emergency stop button on the winch? Why didn't he even wear a life jacket? I beat my fist on the wheel.

"Grandpa, the radio. How does it work?" I shouted.

He moaned a few words, but it was just a muddle. The ball of fabric around his arm was starting to turn red.

The sea was getting rougher. I kept having to get up and adjust our course, and I was drenched by the rain. Then I found Grandpa's oilskins in the cabin. Shivering, I spread out the oilskin jacket on top of all the blankets. When I'd finished, Grandpa looked like a mummy. Only the center of his face was visible, but he was still shaking. I put my ear right down by his mouth. He was whispering something. I leaned closer.

"Inger," he murmured, and then it was as if he drifted away again.

I started to cry. Why was he saying Granny's name? Couldn't he see me? Was he dying?

"I'm here, Grandpa," I cried. "I'm here."

Then I had to go back up to the wheel. A prayer

pounded away inside me, over and over again. Let Grandpa live. Let Grandpa stay with me. Make Grandpa wake up. Make Grandpa better. Let him stay with me.

The town emerged above the misty sea now and then. It was getting closer and closer, but we didn't meet a single other boat. Nobody could help me. *Troll* was pummeling against the waves and struggling through the sea, Grandpa was breathing and bleeding, and I was praying and crying. Oh, if only the engine had that extra horsepower Lena had talked about! It was so slow that it hurt.

It's hard to say what he made of it all, that sun-tanned man in the white sailboat who was the first to see us. He probably thought about his own boat first, as here came a fishing boat roaring into the town harbor with a half-crazed boy for a skipper.

"Help!" I shouted, waving my arms. "You've got to call an ambulance. Grandpa's hurt!"

Then I did what made Grandpa proudest of all. I docked the boat. I didn't smash any sailboats. I didn't give *Troll* so much as a single scratch either, which clearly surpassed everything else I'd done that day.

"Old *Troll* is no easy boat to maneuver and berth, you know," Grandpa said later, as if that was what made me the hero of the day.

"Pure luck," was what Lena had to say about the docking. "Pure, sheer luck."

Part Four

Spring Is Sprung

CHAPTER THIRTY-THREE

After the Accident

*I*t was so strange to be somebody else all of a sudden. I was no longer that snotty brat from Mathildewick Cove. Now I was the boy who'd saved his grandfather's life.

Magnus stopped making fun of me, Mom cried at the very sight of me, and the old men at the shop said hello to me as if I were a grown man.

"I always thought that Mini-Lars had the right stuff," I caught the hard-of-hearing Thunderclap Kåre telling Pitt one day as I was going past.

They even wrote about me in the newspaper.

But I don't think I really understood what a big thing I'd done until I heard Dad talk about it. The

Sunday after the accident, he invited Uncle Tor to dinner, as well as everybody from next door. I was in the kitchen with him while he was preparing the meal. He was stirring the pot of chicken fricassee and scurrying around in an apron that was far too small for his stomach.

"Trille," he suddenly said, nodding in the direction of the sea, "what you did for Grandpa . . ."

I looked up in shock. Dad never normally gives me praise. Now he was staring at me as he searched for words, emotion written all over his face.

"I've always been proud of you, but what you did . . . You're a good lad, Trille."

"Do you think so?" I said, stunned.

Dad nodded and fumbled with the whisk, without saying another word. I ran off happily to put the napkins on the kitchen table. In my confusion, I laid a place for Grandpa too.

He'd been moved from the hospital to the nursing home now. I'd ridden my bike over there after breakfast. All the blood loss had made him feel weak and miserable, and his arm was never going to be quite the same again. When I'd gotten there, he was asleep in bed. For as long as I could remember, Grandpa had looked after me. With him I'd always been as safe as a seagull chick. Now it almost felt as if I had to look after him. I sat down quietly on the chair next to the bed. After a while, he woke up a little. A frail smile appeared.

"To think you docked *Troll* all on your own, Trille lad."

And then he fell asleep again.

And now I'd laid him a place at the kitchen table out of habit. I just left it like that. He wasn't dead, after all. I looked at the table, which was all set. At each end, bottles of red-currant squash sparkled in the low February sunlight, and from the middle of the table, wisps of steam curled up from our biggest cast-iron pot. Dad and I looked proudly at each other.

"I would like to propose a toast to Number Seven," Lena said with a cough when everybody had arrived. "Mathildewick Cove's Formula One chicken, who sadly had to die far too young . . ."

"She wasn't all that young," Dad muttered, but he raised his glass anyway.

"And to Trille," said Minda. "The world's littlest lifesaver."

Then we ate the chicken fricassee, the one just like Granny used to make. And just like her parents had surely made for her out on Kobbholmen. Oh, how I wished Birgit could've been there to see it. How could I explain to her that it wasn't just any old dead chicken that had dropped out of midair? And had she heard about Grandpa? I knew I had to go up to Hillside later that evening.

"Can we put some chicken fricassee in a box and take it to the nursing home?" Lena asked when we'd finished tucking in to our dessert and people were about to leave. "It was Lars who provided the main ingredient, after all."

Dad said he'd been about to suggest the same thing, and he poured the leftovers into a huge plastic tub.

Lena and I fetched our bikes. When we got up to the main road, I strapped the tub onto Lena's carrier rack.

"You go," I said. "I went this morning."

Lena frowned and was about to say something, but I was already on my way up the hill.

And so it was that we each went our own way that evening. Lena cycled to the nursing home, and I pedaled all the way up to Birgit at Hillside. The same thing would happen a number of times over the next couple of months.

Spring was sprouting. Bristly yellow dandelions shot up like stars on the edge of ditches. The sea glittered, and even a few shining wood anemones popped out amid all the dead grass on a slope halfway up to Hillside. I saw more and more of them as the days went by, as I was always going to see Birgit and her family. I was almost starting to get used to vegetarian food. After the accident, I could finally talk with her normally again. The episode with the hen hardly mattered anymore once we'd even had a little laugh about it.

Things were different at school too. The day after the rescue, I'd turned up in my wellies. I didn't mind if I looked stupid. I was fed up with having wet feet. In any case, I couldn't give a shark's tail what Kai-Tommy thought. He could just go ahead and stare.

Everything seemed to be going a bit better, except in one place: back home in Mathildewick Cove.

I don't really know what I'd expected to happen when Grandpa finally came home. I suppose I'd imagined we'd sit down in his apartment and talk about the accident, shaking our heads as we thought about the giant halibut and those dramatic few hours. At the least I thought Grandpa would look at me warmly and thank me, like Dad had done. But he didn't say anything. It was as if everything with the halibut and the winch hadn't even happened. Instead, Grandpa walked around like a shadow, holding his arm and hunched over in a way I hadn't seen before. Was he angry?

On the very first day of warm sunshine, I asked if he wanted to come along down to the boat shed again. He quickly backed away with his hand over his face, mumbling something about not quite feeling up to it.

"Maybe another day," he added, without looking straight at me.

"All right," I said, trying not to sound down-hearted.

So then I asked another day, but Grandpa said the same thing. I felt a strange emptiness in my stomach. Why didn't he want to spend time with me?

Lena wasn't trampling all over our doormat any-more either. To start with I thought that might be a good thing, but actually it made me sad. She was going to her blasted practices all the time, and when we did meet, she was quiet and morose, not really her usual self.

And then, early one Saturday morning, a few weeks after Grandpa had come home, everything became twice as difficult as before. From my window, I saw Grandpa and Lena walking down to the boat shed together. He was wearing his overalls for the first time since the accident, and she was carrying his toolbox. I could feel tears of anger welling up behind my eyes. Why hadn't they asked if I wanted to come too? I swallowed hard and turned away from the window. Soon I was on my way up to Hillside. They were welcome to have a nice time without me!

I didn't ask Grandpa if he wanted to come along down to the boat shed anymore. But I did discover, to my despair, that many of the times I'd been to Hillside or other places, he and Lena had been down there without me.

CHAPTER THIRTY-FOUR

Rumba Ruin

*I*t's so wonderful this is happening, especially since we couldn't come to the concert at Christmas!" Ylva said happily.

It was May, and some totally crazy person at school, probably the music teacher, had gotten it into their head that the ones in our class who had music school lessons should provide the entertainment at a class party for our parents. I'd actually been unusually angry when Mr. Rognstad told us. I wasn't about to start practicing like I'd done before Christmas. No way, José.

"It's 'Für Elise' or nothing," I'd said, surprised to find that I was able to put my foot down this time.

Ylva, who had been feeling sick for the first few months with the baby in her stomach, was sparkling as she sat next to me. I've always thought Lena has the prettiest mom. She has long, dark hair and a silver nose stud. Now she was prettier than ever: she was shining. She was holding Isak's hand, and her other hand was lying over her baby bump. Imagine being so happy just about going to a concert.

I peered over at Lena. She was sitting there, gloomily staring straight ahead. I knew that she'd been practicing. I'd heard the booming rhythms of the keyboard through the walls of her house many times over the past week. The question was whether it had helped.

The lights had been dimmed in the school auditorium, which was full of friends and families. I'd finished "Für Elise," and Krølla had clapped with great gusto. Now it was Lena's turn. She was wearing a dress, and her hair was neatly braided. I hadn't seen her in a dress since Isak and Ylva got married. For the first time, it struck me that she looked a bit like Ylva.

Then my neighbor hurled the keyboard volume up

to full and switched on some absurd rumba rhythm. It was clear that she'd decided to go down fighting. But she made it all the way through the piece, in her own way, with a lot of pauses and strange noises. I could see how much she hated every single note. When she'd finished, she rushed straight offstage and sat down next to Andreas instead of us. I glanced cautiously at Ylva. She tried to wave to Lena to get her to come and join us, but it was no use. Lena sat there, staring angrily at her shoes, while Birgit dazzled her way through a kind of jazz piece that left most people's mouths open in admiration.

After the concert, we waited for our parents in the parking lot.

"That wasn't too bad, really," I said.

Lena pulled uncomfortably at her dress and gave me a sullen look.

"I've got a game tomorrow. Two o'clock. Are you coming to watch, or what?" she said, a little irritably.

"Your first game in town?" I asked.

She nodded. It was a long time since I'd last seen Lena in goal. And it was a long time since she'd invited me to anything. I felt confused and happy in an unexpected way. I was about to say yes when Birgit suddenly appeared.

"Hi," she said. "It's my birthday tomorrow. Would you two like to come to my house at around three o'clock?"

"Um . . . sure," I said.

Lena looked at me more or less in the same way as she had that time I spilled the beans to Birgit about the raft.

"What about you, Lena?" Birgit asked.

Lena didn't say a word in reply. She just turned around and left. That's when I became angry. Railing rams, there's a limit. I ran after her.

"What's your problem, Lena?"

She didn't answer.

"Do you think I should miss a birthday party just to see a totally normal soccer game?"

Lena stopped. "I couldn't care less what you do! It's your life!" she said.

"Yes, it is, actually!" I shouted. "And I'm absolutely sick and tired of you being grumpy all the time."

"Grumpy?" said Lena in disbelief. "I'll tell you one thing, Trille Danielsen Yttergård: it's better to be grumpy than to be an idiot."

She threw her keyboard book into the ditch, sending mud splashing out, and ran off home.

"Kai-Tommy's right," I yelled after her. "You've got serious problems with your temper!"

Back at home, I went straight up to my room. I was furious. For a moment I thought about going down to Grandpa in the boat shed. But then I saw that Lena was already there. That made me even angrier. What were they doing together? Couldn't she get her own grandpa? I spotted the ice-cream tub with the broken bottle and ship in it on my shelf. I tore it down in rage and emptied all the contents into the garbage can by the toilet.

CHAPTER THIRTY-FIVE

"My Boat Is So Small"

*B*irgit's family had set out a long table in their barn. The walls were decorated with paper lanterns, and there were bunches of spring flowers everywhere. The table was teeming with colorful foods, not bread and sausages like we were used to. It was like stepping into a film. All the boys from class were being polite and trying to behave maturely.

Birgit was wearing a light-blue dress and a necklace of polished wooden beads. Her curls softly touched my face as she gave me a hug.

"Happy birthday," I murmured dizzily. "Nice necklace."

"Keisha gave it to me." Birgit put her hand on the beads, clearly pleased with it. "She sent it for my birthday."

Andreas and Abdulahi came in after me. They got hugs too. Kai-Tommy was already on the ramp at the entrance to the barn, chatting confidently with Birgit's father, the author. He was wearing a shirt like the one his brother had been wearing at Christmas.

"Wh-where's Lena?" Andreas asked. He was looking nervously at a tray of stuffed mushrooms.

"She's playing a game in town," I grumbled. The very thought of Lena made my stomach boil with rage.

From the corner of my eye, I spotted Birgit sitting down on the bottom step of the barn and talking with Kai-Tommy. They sat there for quite a while. She laughed several times. I'd managed to eat a whole load of those mushrooms before they got up. I suddenly felt that I just wanted to go home. All the small talk and all the people—I just couldn't cope. I quietly told Birgit that I had a headache and shuffled off down the hill.

Down at the bend with the wood anemones, I stopped and looked out across the fjord. It was still and light blue in the afternoon sun. A small plastic-hulled boat was on its way out. "My boat is so small and your sea is so wide." We'd learned that song at Sunday school. I watched the boat and the lone wake behind it. That was exactly how I felt.

I lay in my room, looking at the picture I'd been given for Christmas. Birgit had painted Kobbholmen and *Troll* and the beautiful summer colors with her own hands. What did I normally think about before Birgit came along with her curls?

I don't know how long I'd been lying there when there was a knock at my door.

"Trille?" Mom stuck her head around. "Ylva's downstairs. She's wondering if you know where Lena is."

"Isn't she at the soccer game?" I asked.

No, the game had finished several hours ago, Mom told me. Nobody had seen Lena all day.

I went down to the kitchen.

"Weren't you at the game either?" I asked, looking at Ylva, who was reading a message on her phone.

"No, I couldn't face it, Trille. I felt so nauseous, and . . ."

"What about Isak?" asked Mom, bobbing up and down a little to calm Inger.

"Isak's on call today. I can't get hold of him either," said Ylva.

A painful feeling crept into my chest. "Did nobody go to watch her play?"

Ylva looked at me. She was forlorn, and I knew a painful feeling had crept into her chest too. Lena's first game, and nobody to cheer her on.

"I'll check with Grandpa," I said, heading out.

What nonsense was Lena up to now? Couldn't she see that people were getting fed up with everything having to be about soccer all the time? She hadn't even replied to Birgit when she'd invited her to her party. Actually, now that I thought about it properly, she was being really selfish. I stuck my hands in my pockets as I strode across the fields.

Grandpa was standing at the door when I arrived at the boat shed. I peered over his shoulder. There were all sorts of odds and ends in there, and it struck me that Lena must have been gathering bits of flotsam and jetsam for a new raft all spring.

"Have you seen Lena?" I asked.

"No."

I explained what Mom had said. From the corner of my eye, I noticed Isak's car turning in to the farmyard back up by the house.

Grandpa scratched his head a little. "Then it must be Lena who's taken it," he said. "But how on earth did she manage that?"

He disappeared into the old boat shed.

"Manage what?"

"The boat's gone," said Grandpa.

What did he mean? Both *Troll* and Dad's blue plastic-hulled boat were at the floating pier inside the breakwater. They certainly weren't gone.

"Which boat?"

Grandpa glanced at me. "Your boat."

"I haven't got a boat, Grandpa," I said quietly.

Was that why he'd been so strange recently? Had he started getting confused?

"Grandpa, I haven't got a boat," I said again, in despair.

Grandpa turned toward me. "No, you haven't, Trille, but you were going to get one."

He drummed his fingers pensively against the wall of the boat shed.

"Lena and I have been fixing up an old Silver Viking for you, here in the old boat shed. It was supposed to be a surprise for your birthday."

What?

Grandpa pushed open the doors that led out to the water.

"Lena and I thought it was about time you had your own boat. You deserved it after . . . Well, you know."

He patted his injured arm and gave me a sheepish look.

A boat for me? From Grandpa and Lena? Was that what they'd been doing during all those hours together down by the boat sheds? Fixing up a boat? For me?

Overwhelmed, I stared across the rocks by the shore. There were clear traces of somebody having taken out a boat. The rollers for moving it were strewn all the way down to the water's edge. I knew how strong Lena could be when she was angry and upset. She would've needed a lot of strength for this.

"Grandpa, we've got to find her!" I shouted.

At that very moment, Isak came bounding down across the fields.

"Do you know where she is?" There was an unusual quiver in his normally calm voice.

"No, but we'll soon find out," said Grandpa. "Fetch your life jacket, Trille, then . . ."

He took a deep breath.

"Then we'll launch *Troll*."

CHAPTER THIRTY-SIX

A Desperate Dad

I held my breath as I stood on deck, watching Grandpa turn on the boat's ignition for the first time since the accident. It had been a while, and *Troll* coughed and shook a few times, but soon the engine was throbbing in its happy, familiar way. Isak untied the last mooring line and leaped on board, and then we put out to sea.

To begin with, Grandpa looked as stiff as a statue, but gradually it was as if the shuddering engine shook out the old Grandpa. He checked a little bit, adjusted a little bit, squinted a little bit. But mostly he stood there with his arm firmly and calmly on the wheel, peering out to sea with blue eyes.

Suddenly, I realized how quiet it had been the last few months. I leaned against the railing and felt the engine throbbing throughout my body. It was as if my pulse were back.

Isak was peering all around. "I didn't manage to talk to her after the game. I had an emergency call . . ."

"Were you at the game?"

Isak nodded. He'd seen almost the whole thing, he said, but then he'd had to leave a short while before the end.

"I don't think Lena could see me, though, because I had to stay up by the car in case I got a call."

He was staring everywhere.

"Was she good?" I asked.

Isak turned to look at me. "Good? She was outstanding, Trille. I had no idea that she was so good. Did you know?"

I gulped. Lena, Lena. Where was she?

Grandpa had set course toward the mouth of the fjord. Neither Isak nor I had objected. We knew Lena. She wasn't the sort to nip over to town when she was upset. It was more her style to point straight out to sea.

"She's probably on her way to Crete or something," said Grandpa, trying to get us to smile. It didn't work. Isak's face was completely gray. I'd never seen him like that.

We sailed on for a while without saying anything.

"Are you sure that she's gone this way?" Isak asked eventually. He was so restless now that he couldn't stand still.

Grandpa shook his head.

"Maybe we should turn around and look . . ."

Isak didn't get any further. All three of us saw it at the same moment. A small boat floating in the sea. Bright white in the afternoon light, with freshly painted green boards to sit on. My boat.

Totally empty.

Now I know what a terrified dad calling out for his child sounds like. Isak was shouting so much that I thought his heart would tear.

"Lena!" he yelled out across the still waters. *"Lena!"*

I didn't call her name. I couldn't even look at the

white boat. Feeling powerless, I sat down on deck and stared at Grandpa's boots.

"We've got to alert . . . We've got to . . ." Isak stammered, fumbling with his phone. "Lena!" he called out again.

"Just hold on a moment there, Isak," said Grandpa, pointing at the horizon. "Lena might be all right."

A thin plume of smoke was rising up from Kobbholmen.

We could see her from some distance. She was standing motionless on the old pier, still wearing her soccer cleats and tracksuit. Her black hair was hanging over her face, and her fists were clenched. Isak jumped ashore when we still had a few feet to go. He reached her in two quick bounds and lifted her up like a feather. Nothing happened at first, but then Lena started crying. She cried and cried, and Isak held on to her tightly until the crying faded.

Then Grandpa turned off the engine and nodded at the bonfire. "Are you cooking hot dogs?"

Lena wiped her eyes with her sleeve and nodded.

"Are there any left?"

Lena nodded again.

I realized she must've had some kind of plan to live on Kobbholmen. She'd packed food and a sleeping bag. She told us that she'd pushed the boat away herself so she wouldn't be tempted to go home immediately.

"But why don't you want to go home?" Isak asked quietly.

Lena didn't answer. She just poked at her beautiful bonfire and was as silent as a dead crab.

"Lena?"

"Because nobody likes me," she said eventually.

Grandpa, Isak, and I all stared at her in shock. Nobody liked her?

"But, Lena . . ." Isak looked at her, brokenhearted. "How can you say that?"

"Because it's true," she muttered.

"No, it's not true," said Isak.

Lena turned one of the logs on the fire, sending smoke and embers hissing into the sky.

"Well, I'm not the way you want me to be. So I might as well live out here."

"You're exactly the way we want you to be —" Isak began.

But Lena became enraged. "No, I'm not," she said. "There's not a soul who cares about what I can do. But as for music and math and all that rubbish I can't do . . . You all think those things are a matter of life and death."

She raked the fire angrily.

"Shrieking sharks, I don't want to be stuck hanging around in Mathildewick Cove like some kind of keyboard-playing Christmas decoration."

Isak was about to answer, but before he could, Lena started crying again.

"You and Mom haven't been to see a single flipping soccer game in all my life, and Trille . . ."

She didn't say any more.

I looked at her sadly. Isak put his arm around Lena and told her he had been at the game. He'd seen that penalty she'd saved. He'd heard Lena taking charge of the back line, directing them and keeping them in order even though it was her first game. And he'd seen how quick and focused she was right from the start of the game. He'd heard the other girls, who were two years older than she was, calling to her and singing her praises. And he'd had to leave five minutes before the end, because there was a young man on the other side of town who'd had a heart attack.

Lena wiped her hand across her eyes and looked at him in disbelief.

"You saw the penalty?" she asked breathlessly.

Isak nodded.

"Did you see how she tried to make it look like she was going to shoot to the left, but I threw myself to the right anyway because . . ."

"I saw," said Isak.

Lena sat up straight. She had a strange expression on her face.

"But Isak, did you see . . ."

"I saw everything," Isak said, smiling. "I was the proudest dad of the whole game."

On the way home, we picked up the little white boat and towed it along. Lena was behind my back, but I could tell she was looking at me. I hadn't managed to say a word the whole time.

When we were on our way back up from the boat
sheds, and I was dragging my feet under the rowan
trees, she stopped and waited for me.

"Trille?"

I gulped.

"Shall we try out your boat tomorrow?"

I nodded.

CHAPTER THIRTY-SEVEN

A Serious Talk – and a Few Mackerel Too

It's a funny thing with Lena. As we pushed off from shore on my boat at the crack of dawn the next morning, it was as if there'd never been any problem at all.

"Isn't it a top-notch boat, Trille? It was Lars who fixed the outboard motor."

I leaned over and pulled the cord. The engine started on the first pull, and soon we were speeding along. It was a fantastic boat. But I just couldn't cheer myself up. I felt a great lump in my throat at the very thought that this was my boat. I didn't deserve it.

When we stopped the boat and Lena wanted to start fishing, I took a deep breath.

"Lena, I'm sorry that . . ."

Lena just waved her hand. "I'm sorry too, and all that stuff."

I smiled slightly, but I felt I wasn't finished. It wasn't that simple.

"It's just that I like to be with other people too sometimes," I began.

Lena sighed. "Well, obviously. You just don't get it, do you?"

Clearly not, I thought, surprised to see that she was already managing to get on my nerves again.

"I don't want to spend all my time with you either," she said. "Smoking haddocks, that would be quite a burden," she added.

Oh, she was so . . . ! I started to prepare my fishing line. We didn't say anything for a long while, and then it was Lena who took a deep breath.

"The thing is, Trille, it must be possible to fall in love without turning into a blinking idiot while you're at it."

"Fall in love?" I said. "I'm not in love."

"Just an idiot?"

"Huh?"

"Who knows, maybe I could even have helped you."

"Helped me?"

"Yes. Can't you see how hopeless it is to go on playing the piano when you hate it? Or to sit at the ferry landing like a nitwit? For cod's sake. Do you think that's going to entice any ladies?"

"But . . ."

"If Birgit has *any* sense in that head of hers — and we may very well wonder if she does, actually — then she'll see that you're the best one of all."

"Huh?"

Lena didn't say any more for a while. She brushed some dirt off her overalls and sighed.

"I also think it would be good for your mental health if you took up playing the drums," she said in conclusion.

"You're deranged," I said.

"Thanks, you too," Lena grumbled, giving me one of her smiles that would make the grayest of rocks glitter.

I felt something melt inside me, and I started

laughing. Lena sat there for a while, looking at me with a cheery glint in her eye, and then she broke down too. We laughed and laughed. We almost laughed our way to Davy Jones's locker, both of us.

When we'd finally calmed down, we cast our lines and started fishing. The mackerel had arrived now, and it wasn't long before the lines were twitching and thrashing around on both sides of the boat.

After we'd gotten back from Kobbholmen the day before, I'd been down to the water all by myself. Nets and fishing lines were hung throughout the boat shed in meticulous order. None of them had been in the water since Grandpa hurt his hand. Up in the boat shed loft, I'd found the box with the damaged halibut line in it. I'd taken it down, lit the lamp above Grandpa's stool, and sat there, unraveling and mending it until late in the evening. Now it was in the wooden box, ready to be used. The only thing missing was some decent bait.

Lena and I sorted that out. The tub between us was soon full of mackerel. Enough to bait plenty of lines.

"Do you think we'll get Grandpa out line fishing next weekend?" I asked.

Lena shrugged and suddenly looked serious.

"After all, we finally got him back at sea yesterday, didn't we?" I said, feeling a little uncertain.

Lena glanced at me.

"What is it?" I eventually asked.

"I think maybe Lars is worried he won't manage all this fishing anymore, Trille, what with his hand and everything," Lena said. "He's starting to get old, you know," she added.

It felt like a wall had crumbled inside me. Grandpa didn't have anything to be worried about, did he? Images of the giant halibut and all the blood flickered past my eyes. I looked back to shore. Grandpa was up in the farmyard. He was pulling Inger's stroller back and forth with his good arm while looking out at Lena and me.

CHAPTER THIRTY-EIGHT

"Who Do You Like Best?"

J was thinking about maybe going to the game this afternoon," I said to Lena when we'd moored the boat and sorted out the fish.

The boys from our class were playing their first game of the summer season. Kai-Tommy had been talking about it for ages. They were playing against the team from town, which had won the league by a mile the year before. But the boys at school had been training hard all winter. Kai-Tommy thought they were going to win. The league title too! I knew that Birgit would be there watching.

"Sounds good," said Lena, grabbing hold of her side of the fish tub. "But I've got practice to go to."

And so it was. Lena sped off on her bike, and I went to the game. I watched her as she cycled away, feeling a warmth in my chest that hadn't been there for a long time. Lena Lid, my best friend and neighbor. There wasn't another person in the world like her.

When I arrived at the field, I saw Axel and Ellisiv sitting in the stands, so I went and joined them.

"Now I can safely say that I've got a girlfriend," said Axel.

Ellisiv rolled her eyes and made space for me. Down on the field, my classmates ran back and forth as they warmed up. I looked around anxiously for Birgit. It took me a while to spot her sitting alone at the far end of the stands.

She looked up in surprise when I reached her.

"Hi, Trille! Are you feeling better?"

"Huh? Oh, you mean . . . Yes, it passed quickly. Was it a good party?"

Birgit nodded and looked out across the field. Was she watching Kai-Tommy?

"It was a bit sad too."

"Sad?"

"Yes, we're going back home to Amsterdam soon, you know."

She said she'd known the whole time that they were only here for a year, but she'd thought it would be all right.

"I remembered what it felt like leaving Keisha in Kenya, so I'd really decided not to make such good friends here."

I sat down.

"It's very difficult not to grow fond of people," she said. "Do you know what I mean?"

I nodded. Who understood that better than me? I was about to say something when a shadow fell over us.

It was Kai-Tommy, slightly out of breath, with his dark bangs and bright-blue uniform.

"Hi, so good you made it," he said to Birgit.

He looked at me nervously, and it suddenly dawned on me that Kai-Tommy felt just as worked up seeing me talking with Birgit as I did when he talked with her.

"Where did you leave Lena, then?" he asked me.

"She's practicing in town."

He sighed in annoyance. "She never gives up. Somebody should tell her that she hasn't exactly got a goalkeeper's body, the skinny sardine that she is."

I was about to say something back, but I couldn't be bothered. It was better just to leave it.

"Talk to you later, then!" he said, running off.

"Do you like Kai-Tommy, really?" I blurted out. I needed to know.

Birgit looked at me in confusion. "Yes, quite a lot."

"But . . ." I flung out my arms, baffled.

"He's nice deep down, Trille."

It had to be pretty deep down, I thought.

"I like you a lot too, you know," she added.

A warm feeling ran through my body. "Who do you like best, then?" I tried to make it sound like a silly question.

Birgit laughed. She looked at the boys, who'd formed two huddles out on the field. Then she became serious.

"Well, probably Keisha," she said quietly, with a lopsided smile.

I didn't know what else to say. Birgit was going to leave soon. The thought was unbearable, but it was good to sit there with her, for the moment.

"I'll miss you," I finally managed to say.

"I'll miss you too, Trille."

And then the game started.

CHAPTER THIRTY-NINE

The Guys on the Field

The game turned out to be one nobody would forget in a hurry. The red team from town put the pressure on from the start, but our local team stayed solid at the back, blocking all their attacks. It was clear that a lot had changed over the winter. Ivar obviously knew what he was doing, whatever Lena thought about him.

It was no more than a couple of minutes into the game when Andreas made a long pass to Abdulahi, who brought the ball down and shot it at the other team's goal. The goalie from town barely managed to throw himself down in time and smack the ball away.

Then it was the team from town on the offensive. Halvor punched the ball just off the field, and a corner was awarded. He stopped the ball again, and reluctantly I had to admit that he was starting to turn into a good keeper. I was seriously impressed with my classmates. They managed to get past midfield time after time. The red team's defense had their work cut out for them stopping the attacks. Several times it was only their goalie, dressed in black, who saved them from going a goal down.

Birgit was on her feet. "Come on!" she shouted.

When the ball went off for a throw-in, I cast my eyes over the spectators. Minda and Magnus and their friends were sitting at the top of the stands. Ellisiv and Axel were both on their feet, cheering. There were people I knew all the way along the touchline. And what in heaven's name? Ylva! She was standing down by the other team's corner post, looking totally confused. I sighed in despair. This was so typical of her! After the previous day's drama, she'd probably decided that she was finally going to start coming to Lena's games but hadn't remembered that Lena had changed teams! Was it possible? I slapped my forehead.

The goalie from town, in his black shirt, put the ball down at the edge of the goal area, took aim, and kicked it in a precise arc. The ball crossed the field and landed smack bang at the feet of an unmarked player just over the center line. Before we knew it, the boy in red had fended off two defenders and shot the ball into the back of the net. We were down one–nil!

The audience sighed and booed. The away team clapped, of course, but I could hear one person above all the rest, screaming with joy down by the corner post. It was Ylva. She was cheering on the wrong team! Lena would've had a fit.

"Sorry, I'll be back in a bit," I said to Birgit, hurrying down to the touchline. I couldn't let Ylva carry on making a fool of herself like that!

I'd almost reached Ylva when I looked again at the little goalie from town in his black shirt. He was standing there calmly, a short distance out into the penalty box, waiting for the game to get started again. He had his cap pulled down low, as he was facing straight into the sun. Every now and then he pointed and shouted something to the red team's defenders, with a slightly delicate but determined voice. I opened my mouth and then closed it again. No . . . it couldn't be!

The game was back on, and the little goalie bobbed up and down on his toes, full of concentration. He moved to the side, keeping an eagle eye on the ball. Then he brought one of his gloves up to his mouth and yelled at two of the players in red:

"Hello! Time to wake up and smell the waffles over there! Keep an eye on number ten!"

I practically collapsed there and then.

Lena!

And what happened next was something I'll never forget. While I was still standing there, slightly in shock, the player in the blue number-ten shirt, Kai-Tommy, stole the ball from the attacking town side. He turned with it and ran. Two red players behind him tried to catch up, but they were too slow. Kai-Tommy was storming forward at a furious speed. It was him against the keeper.

The player in black, with the cap on her head, moved back closer and closer to the goal. Then, just when everybody was sure it was about to turn one–all, the little sardine suddenly started to run forward.

"Come on!" Ylva shouted behind me.

With great precision, Lena fearlessly threw herself down onto the gravel just inside the penalty area, grabbing the ball from under the feet of the lone striker. Kai-Tommy fell forward, and Lena rolled a couple of times as she held the ball tightly, as if it were a precious egg. It was a textbook tackle. And it was pretty impressively done.

An enraged Kai-Tommy got back on his feet. He was about to yell something when he saw the same thing I'd seen. If only I could describe the look on his face. It was like he'd been run over by a UFO.

"So good to get to play at the right level now and then," Lena said dryly, courteously doffing her cap.

Then she turned back to the game as if nothing had happened.

*　*　*

The team from town completely dominated the rest of the game and took three well-deserved points home with them on the ferry. But the player of the game stayed behind, waving at them as they left.

People talked about that game for a long time afterward. When they realized what had happened—that Ivar and the boys had more or less forced Lena off their team—many were angry. But Lena wasn't angry anymore. Changing teams was one of the best things that had ever happened to her. She liked playing with the girls, and since the coach in town had quickly spotted her talent, she was constantly being asked if the boys' team could borrow her too.

But she didn't always say yes.

"I can't play soccer every day," she explained. "I've got quite a lot to be getting on with at home too, after all."

I knew she was thinking about that raft.

CHAPTER FORTY

Grandpa and Thunderclap Kåre

J 've ordered an emergency stop button for the winch," Dad said softly as he cut a couple of thick slices of bread.

"Oh," I said.

We were eating breakfast at the kitchen counter. It was Saturday, and the sun was shining. The boat traffic was in full swing out on the fjord, but through the window I could see Grandpa sitting marooned at the table in the yard, drinking his coffee.

Terrible images of the halibut and the blood flew through my head again. Was it the same for Grandpa? I peered at him out in the yard. He looked so lonely. I suddenly realized it was even worse for him.

Dad chewed his bread next to me. "We've got to get the old man out fishing again, Trille. We can't go on like this."

"Is that Thunderclap Kåre out off the headland?" I asked, plonking myself down next to Grandpa.

He nodded, turning his coffee cup round and round in his good hand. Grandpa had always made fun of Thunderclap Kåre for not going out to catch the big fish. Now we could clearly see him hauling up a load of small coalfish.

"Do you know that I once struck him down?" Grandpa said.

"You hit Thunderclap Kåre? Why?"

"He was dancing with Inger." Grandpa shook his head and chuckled. "I was seventeen and just about to go to sea for the first time."

He squinted at Thunderclap Kåre's boat. "It's the most foolish thing I've ever done in my life."

"Were you and Granny already boyfriend and girlfriend when you were seventeen?" I asked, surprised.

"No, we were friends. But that summer, she suddenly came along one day to tell me that she was going to miss me when I left. She even said that she'd gladly wait for me."

Grandpa smiled.

"And what did I do, the idiot that I am? I cheekily turned her down, just like I'd turned down all the others. I didn't want any girl waiting at home for me. I wanted to be footloose and fancy-free."

But the day before Grandpa was due to leave, something happened. There was a dock dance where the ferry landing is now, Grandpa told me. All the young people in the area were gathered there that summer's evening. When he arrived, he saw Inger among all the others. And as if by magic, it dawned on him what he'd done. Holy mackerel, she was the one he really liked!

"And so you hit him?" I asked, shocked.

"You bet I did."

I realized it had been a close call: my grandparents almost hadn't gotten together at all. Granny had been furious. Not only had Grandpa jilted her and made her unhappier than she'd ever been before, he then had the nerve to assault a totally innocent guy who actually liked her. Could anybody be more of a fool? Grandpa had to sail off to Baltimore with a broken heart and a guilty conscience.

I glanced in astonishment at my calm and peaceful grandfather.

"I never would've thought you could punch somebody," I said.

"Oh?" He laughed. "I'm so old now that I know we all do foolish things. It doesn't matter that much, really."

He peered out at Thunderclap Kåre again. "What matters is what we do afterward."

From the corner of my eye, I saw Lena come out onto her doorstep with her soccer ball in her hands. Grandpa spotted her too.

"This world's so well put together, Trille, that most things we mess up can be sorted out again. But sometimes it's a tough job," he added.

Thunderclap Kåre got his outboard motor started and chugged back toward the shore. Lena was already down in the field with her ball.

"Grandpa, today we're going line fishing," I said, making it clear that he had no choice.

CHAPTER FORTY-ONE

The Message in a Bottle

*T*he day Birgit left, it was summer again. Grandpa and I were going fishing almost every day. Back on dry land, Ylva was walking around with a bump as big as the one Mom had been carrying at Christmas. And in the old boat shed, Lena's raft was ready to be launched.

The whole family from Hillside came down to Mathildewick Cove before they left. They had to drop off Haas. Birgit had decided. I knew how fond she was of her dog, and yet she wanted him to stay with Lena. She thought he would be happier here. That's what she was like — and that was why I liked her. Lena had been a bit shocked to receive such a generous gift. I didn't really know what she'd said to Birgit, but I hoped it was thank you.

"Maybe we'll go and study together one day, right?" Birgit said to me before they left.

Maybe we will, I thought. *Who knows, anyway?*

Then I got one last curly-haired hug before the Dutch family drove off between the forest and the sea. I stood there, feeling weak and empty, staring at the car in the distance. Grandpa came and stood next to me. After a while, Lena stuck her head between us and put one hand on my shoulder and one on Grandpa's.

"Well, lads," she said with a smirk. "Now it's just the three of us again."

I could've hit her.

Later that day, we were back down by the shore. Lena was lying on her stomach among the clumps of seaweed, attaching a tow hook to the raft, while Haas sat calmly in the sun, watching.

"Do you seriously think we're going to tow you

all the way out to Kobbholmen?" I asked despair-
ingly, looking at the enormous raft on the pebbles
by the shore. "It'll take all day."

"I've got plenty of time," said Lena, her mouth full
of screws. "I've got to check if this thing's seaworthy,
after all."

I knew it was pointless arguing, so I went into the
old boat shed to find a suitable rope. As I scanned
all the hooks and shelves, I suddenly spotted a bottle
with a piece of paper in it. It was hidden up on a
rafter right inside the shed.

"It's a message in a bottle," said Lena from behind
me. "I found it that day back in the winter when we
were looking for wreckage. When Birgit came back,
you remember?"

Just her name gave me a wistful sinking feeling.

"Who is it from, then?"

"Who do you think?" Lena asked dryly.

I opened the bottle and unrolled the sheet of
paper. It was from us, of course, and yet it felt like it
was from somebody else. Childish writing careened
across the paper.

Deer whoever finds this messidge in a botl we
are too frends from mathildewik cove and our
fone number is . . .

"This is ancient," I said, stunned.

I read it again. My heart beat warmly but pain-
fully in my chest. I pictured Lena and me as we'd
been when we were young. Two good friends in our
welly boots, throwing out messages in bottles just
a few yards from shore, thinking they'd travel the
world.

"I wasn't very good at spelling then," I mumbled,
so Lena wouldn't see that I was almost crying.

Lena could see it anyway. She tilted her head and
gave me a kind look.

"I know. Imagine that, Trille. A gifted child like
you."

Then she started waving a coil of rope impa-
tiently. "Are we going outside, then?"

We put out to sea. Grandpa stood calmly and
slightly stoop-shouldered, squinting as usual. He
had his injured hand in his overall pocket and his

good hand on the wheel. Now and then, he glanced back and chuckled. A giant raft, made from the wreckage of one of the worst hurricanes of all time, was heavily pounding through the sea behind us, its happy owner and ship's dog on board.

"If she bumped into the ferry with that thing, I truly don't know who would sink first," Grandpa grumbled. Then he raised his shoulders slightly and turned toward me.

"Well, time for an old man to have some coffee. Do you want to take over here, Trille?"

He let go of the wheel and stepped aside. A fresh breeze ruffled my hair as I took control. I could still feel the warmth of Grandpa's hand in the wood. Birgit was in the Netherlands, but the ocean lay ahead of me, wide and blue. Far out there, by Kobbholmen, was a fishing line in the sea, exactly where my grandmother had once shown it was a good place to put it. And towed behind us, using the most solid rope in Mathildewick Cove, was my best friend and neighbor on her raft.

"Hey, Trille!" Lena yelled from back there.

She'd gotten to her feet and raised her hand

to her mouth, like she does when she calls to the back line in her team. Her voice carried like an earthquake in all directions. I looked quizzically at her, an old feeling of joy bubbling in my stomach. Lena waved and laughed, and then she shouted with all her might:

"Do you think we can speed this convoy up a bit?"